SA
PILG

Louise Dale

Dragonheart
Publishing

Published in Great Britain in 2004
Dragonheart Publishing, The Grey House, Main Street,
Carlton-on-Trent, Newark, Nottinghamshire NG23 6NW

www.dragonheartpublishing.co.uk

British Cataloguing in Publication Data.
A catalogue record of this book is available from the British Library

ISBN 0 9543773 3 8

Cover painting by Ian R. Ward, Mansfield, Nottinghamshire

The Time Trigger Series:
The Curse of Rocamadour
The Keys of Rome
Millennium Spies
Savage Pilgrims

Typesetting and production by
Richard Joseph Publishers Ltd, PO Box 15, Devon EX38 8ZJ

Printed in Great Britain by Creative Print & Design Group,
Middlesex UB7 0LW

For Hope

Contents

1

Imposter

Sweat glinted on the servant's brow under the flickering stage lights. He knelt before Lord Burgh, waiting for an answer. His bulky torso, awkward beneath the tightness of his puritan collar, seemed more soldier than messenger boy.

Alice frowned. There was something different about this man. His costume was incredibly realistic. He had appeared from nowhere, striding onto the stage, interrupting the action and requesting an urgent reply about people who needed a safe place to worship.

The surprised actors on the stage glanced at one another. His lines were obviously not in the script. This was not supposed to happen.

The actor playing Lord Burgh stared at him in confusion.

"Improvise," muttered Alice under her breath.

"Er . . . er . . . I cannot allow it," said Lord Burgh at last, slamming down his tankard and wiping pig juices from his beard. He cast a nervous glance at the watching school children.

The actor in the puritan costume said nothing. He turned to Alice. For a second, she could have sworn that he'd winked at her.

"Er . . . um . . . *Separatists* cannot worship here!" continued Lord Burgh. He fidgeted crossly. "Do you hear me? It is contrary to the king's wishes. Yes. That's what it is. Now, be gone!" He glared at the new man. "Go away . . . whoever you are!"

Alice watched with interest. The burly messenger

bowed graciously and replaced his wide-brimmed hat.

"Very good, m'lud," he said. Then he turned, looking directly at Alice and spoke again, this time with a different accent. "I reckon I'll do just that."

Alice raised her eyebrows in surprise.

"He's an American," she whispered to Robert. "And I think he's looking straight at us."

"Uh, huh. His lordship and the others don't look too keen on him though," said Robert. "I don't think he was a proper part of the play. It's almost as if he's an imposter. He looks too real, as if he genuinely is from the olden times. And from the way he's grinning at us, I'd say he has deliberately gone up there to get our attention or something."

"Rob..." whispered Alice, looking around to make sure no-one else could hear her.

"Yes?" said Robert.

"You don't think... well... that he could be a time traveller like us, do you?" said Alice. "Maybe he has travelled forwards to our century as part of a time travelling quest and camouflaged himself among the actors."

Robert raised his eyebrows and looked back at the man.

"I think you could be right, Alice." Robert smiled mischievously. "Actually, he looks as if he knows full well that the others are actors. He's playing with them for our benefit... almost teasing them. Mind you, his costume is way better!"

The man jumped off the stage and retreated to the shadows behind the audience. The other actors sighed with relief and resumed their noisy feasting. A minstrel started up his baroque music and the children in the audience turned back to watch the play. All except Alice and Robert.

The American grinned at them and pulled something from inside his jacket. To Alice's surprise, he pushed a tiny piece of folded paper into a gap in the black and white plasterwork that decorated the wall between the timbers of the Great Chamber. Then, he looked from Alice to Robert and touched the brim of his hat in a friendly gesture, before stepping silently behind a tapestry screen.

A bright light flashed behind the screen and a cold wind blew Alice's hair behind her shoulders. For the first time in several months she felt that tingling and sickly feeling churning inside her. It was the feeling she sometimes had when she was time travelling or feeling the power of someone connected with a time travelling quest.

"Woah!" said Robert Davenport. He lowered his voice. "He is definitely a time traveller! I think he just left in a Time Tunnel. That probably means he's a Time Regent. If he's got those kind of powers, he's more powerful than ordinary time travellers like the two of us."

"I think we need to get whatever it is that he just stuffed in the wall. I think it was meant for us," said Alice.

"It could be a trap," said Robert. "He could be one of the evil Time Regents who have turned to the dark side."

Alice shuddered.

"He didn't seem evil," she said.

"I hope you're right," said Robert. "Bad Time Regents are deadly. I wish we could make Time Tunnels though. It's a pity we have to make do with Time Triggers. I wish we could summon tunnels whenever we liked. Tunnel rides look so cool." Robert looked dreamily at Alice. "Maybe one day I'll be more powerful..."

"Time Triggers are powerful enough," said Alice. "They certainly take us safely back through the centuries to exactly where we need to go. Some of those journeys have felt like mega-bad roller-coaster rides as it is! And you know we must only time travel for the good of a quest, when the Spirits of Time direct us, otherwise we'd be doomed. Something nasty usually happens to people who try to use Time Triggers for their own greed."

"But more power would be nice," said Robert darkly.

Alice shrugged. She looked sheepishly around. None of the rest of the class had noticed anything. Everyone was watching the Tudor re-enactment, including Mr Picket, the history teacher. She sidled over towards the partition wall. Very slowly, she winkled out the piece of paper without damaging the plaster.

Robert coughed suddenly and Alice glanced up to find Tessa looking straight at her. The play had finished. Alice shoved the note into the pocket of her school skirt and beamed forcefully at Tessa. The other girl's eyes narrowed.

"What are you up to, Alice Hemstock?" she purred loudly. "Did I see you touching that precious art-work?"

The whole class turned and stared.

"What's going on?" said Mr Picket. "I hope you're *not* touching anything, Alice. Didn't you hear what the guide said when we arrived? Gainsborough Old Hall is a living work of art... one of the best pre-served medieval manor houses in England. That's why we've come on this trip. Please respect the history around you. Your twelve-year-old fingers will make marks that will definitely not enhance the ancient décor."

Alice could feel herself blushing.

"Sorry, Sir," she said, trying not to look at Tessa, who was smirking in front of her giggling gang. "I do respect history. Very much, actually, Sir. We are only what we are because of what has been. We are living tomorrow's history and what we do is destined to alter what will be."

"Umm. Very deep, Alice," said Mr Picket, frowning.

Robert stared at Alice. Tessa and her mates giggled again.

"Come on, Year Seven," shouted Mr Picket. "Let's move on to the kitchens, shall we?"

Robert and Alice hesitated, letting the rest of the class go ahead. Alice stuck her tongue out behind Tessa's back.

"Oh, ignore her," said Robert. "You know what she's like. Waste of oxygen. C'mon. We've got far more important stuff to deal with, like what's on that piece of paper?"

Alice grinned at Robert and unravelled the tattered scrap. They were alone now, in the Great Hall.

"This is very old paper. It feels hand-made," she said. "It's rougher than ours. Oh, look! It's a map."

"What does that old fashioned writing say?" said Robert. "*Basworth church*?"

"B-a-b-worth. Babworth church," said Alice.

"That's where the Separatists used to meet, before they were allowed to worship here at the hall," said a friendly woman's voice.

For the second time, Alice hurriedly screwed up the paper. She turned and smiled at the portly tour guide.

"It's back the way your coach must have come," said the lady. "Babworth is a tiny village on the road between here and the motorway. I expect your driver came right past it on the way from your school in Newark."

"Why do you call the puritans *Separatists*?" said Robert. "That's what the actor said earlier."

"Because they worshipped separately," said the friendly lady, perching on the arm of the great throne. "So they were called Separatists. They didn't agree with the way everybody else said their prayers. They liked to keep everything really strict and simple. Some of them eventually came here to Gainsborough Old Hall when it was sold to new owners who were sympathetic. But most people shunned them because they would not follow the king's wishes. There's a display about it downstairs. In fact, some of those who worshipped here and at Babworth church were among the most famous. William Bradford was one of the leaders when they sailed across the Atlantic Ocean in the *Mayflower*. He became their governor and founded one of the first colonies that would one day become the United States of America. Half died of starvation or plague though . . . if the Indians didn't get them, that is. William Bradford would have been a boy about your age when he met secretly with the others here and at Babworth. Imagine that."

"That all sounds more interesting than looking in the old kitchen. Shall we go and look at the display?" said Robert.

"Be careful on the narrow stairs," said the lady, walking back towards the door to the souvenir shop. She smiled at them and winked. "The corridor is haunted, you know."

"Cool," muttered Robert, looking at the staircase.

"Hang on a minute, Rob," said Alice looking at the map again. "Forget ghosts. This is serious. There's something marked here outside the church at Babworth. Don't you think we're supposed to go there?"

"Could be a problem," said Robert. "When will we get a chance to do that?"

"We could ask Mr Picket if we can stop off there on the way back," said Alice.

"There's a connection with America, isn't there?" said Robert. "Hang on a minute!" His eyes flicked wide open in excitement. "I'm going snowboarding in New England next week. I bet that's not just a coincidence. Do you think we could be about to go on a time travelling quest with these pilgrims?"

Alice smiled weakly. Robert might well be right, but she wasn't going to America with him. She wouldn't be included if the quest involved going there.

"We haven't found a Time Trigger," she said. "Nothing has turned up that is connected with the past that could have the powers of a Trigger. You and I can't travel in time without one."

"What about the map?" said Robert.

Alice turned the paper over in her hands. It seemed very flimsy for a Time Trigger.

"Besides," said Robert. "I'm planning on being a Regent sooner or later, you know. I think that's my destiny."

"Oh, yeah?" said Alice, looking at Robert. He smirked arrogantly at her.

"Yeah!"

"You're very sure of yourself, Rob."

"If you want to be big, you have to think big," said Robert.

Alice frowned. Robert's blue eyes danced wildly.

"You worry me sometimes," said Alice.

A dangerous look flashed across Robert's face and for a second, Alice felt a kiss of fear pass over her like a shadow.

She shook her head and looked back at the map.

"Just a minute..." she said. "What if this mark in the church yard is where there's a Time Trigger?"

A big grin spread across Robert's face. He flicked his blond fringe and punched Alice warmly.

"Then we have to persuade Mr Picket to let us stop there," he said.

"Stop where?" said their teacher, leading the class back through the stone archway.

Alice told Mr Picket what the guide had said about the pilgrims and where they'd worshipped before fleeing to America.

"Excellent, Alice and Robert. Well done. Pity more of you can't demonstrate such skills in research," said Mr Picket. "A fine example of history on our doorstep. I think initiative deserves reward. We will take a detour to investigate this church on the way back. Then you can all start a project on the Pilgrim Fathers when we get back to school."

There was a general groan from the rest of the class and Tessa gave Alice an especially poisonous glare. But Robert was smiling.

2

Babworth Ghosts

Robert clicked his new gadget pen from the souvenir shop at Gainsborough Old Hall.

"O.K. I've seen that enough times," said Alice, looking out of the coach window. "It's not a real Trigger or anything."

Robert clicked it once more and grinned.

"We're going to have to sneak away from this lot when we get to the church," he said.

Alice nodded.

"How are we going to dig?" said Robert.

"How do you know we'll need to dig?" said Alice. "The Trigger...if there is one...might be on a grave stone or something."

Robert considered this.

"Suppose so. It's getting a bit dark too. But..."

He produced a small torch from inside his blazer.

Alice shook her head and smiled. The coach turned sharply from the main road and stopped in a rough lay-by.

"O.K.," said Mr Picket. "Babworth church is down this lane behind the trees."

"Do we all have to come, Sir?" said Tessa, sighing.

"No. I suppose not," said Mr Picket. "Those of you who think you'll be bored might as well stay here. We won't be long. And I don't want any more moaning. Those who want to see where real history happened, follow me! It's getting dark quickly now. It will be the shortest day soon, actually."

Mr Picket clomped down the coach steps, still muttering quietly to himself something about British wintertime. Alice, Robert and a dozen of the class followed their energetic teacher into the dusky lane. An owl hooted in the tall pines ahead.

The air was still. All sound stopped, except the noise of their shoes on the dirt track that was once a turning off the Great North Road. A grey mist hung in the trees. Alice heard a thundering sound. She turned, half afraid of what she might see, but it was only a horse running up to look at them in the neighbouring field. Alice looked up. The overarching sycamores that closed around them were the descendants of the mighty Sherwood Forest that once harboured highwaymen and merrymen. The trees whispered in the twilight, witnesses to yet more pilgrims on the path to the church. Then Alice heard another sound. It was like a drum. Voices chanted, quietly at first, then the rhythmic sounds grew louder, calling her from the trees.

"Do you hear them?" she said to Robert.

"What?"

"The drum beat and the voices?"

Robert looked at Alice blankly. She covered her ears. The song was still there, inside her head. It was a gentle chanting from another world, wild and comforting at the same time.

They rounded the bend and stopped. Babworth church greeted them like a giant in the mists. The song in Alice's head stopped dead.

"Here it is," said Mr Picket. "A simple church in an English wood where once young men met up, men who would cross the sea and change the world. I wonder what the Americans make of it? Lots come here to see where their ancestors came from. I've seen expensive tours advertised on the Internet."

He unlatched the iron gates in the low perimeter wall and walked up the path around the church.

Alice opened the old piece of paper.
"Shine that torch here, would you," she said to Robert.
"Told you this would come in handy," said Robert as he flicked the switch.
Alice started humming the *James Bond* theme tune and Robert thumped her. Golden light beamed onto the drawing. The outline of the church was drawn in wobbly black ink, with a faint line representing the archway of the heavy oak doors.
"That must be the clock," said Robert, pointing to a circular marking which corresponded to the old brass clock, forever stuck at ten to two.
"This other mark . . . that's about here," said Robert, pacing to his right between the gravestones. He crouched down and started pushing the grass away with his hands.
"Nothing."
Alice walked slowly in a circle around where Robert sat. Dogs barked in the distance and they could hear their classmates muttering on the other side of the church. Alice shivered.
"There's nothing here," she said. "It's cold, dark, creepy and empty. Good place to come to sense history though. I can almost hear the puritans coming down the lane to meet in secret. Bet it hasn't changed much in the four hundred years since they were here."
"Umm. Must have been a long walk from wherever they lived," said Robert. "Miles and miles. I'm glad we have cars and bikes these days."
"Oh, Rob. What does this paper mean?" said Alice. She was beginning to despair. "Why would that time traveller come to Gainsborough Hall to give it to us? What's here?"
Then she saw it.

"Wait! Over there on the wall. Beneath the clock. Do you see it?"

She leapt across to the church wall. The thick grey bricks were very irregular. About two metres up, there was a round stone. Its inscription had long since been eroded. On the ledge at the base of the stone was a small bundle. Alice jumped up but she couldn't quite reach it.

"Here. I'll lift you," said Robert.

He pushed Alice up, like a skater posing with his partner.

"Ow! No! Stop, Rob!"

Robert lowered Alice to the ground.

"You're pushing me against the wall like that. Piggy back," said Alice.

She jumped on Robert's back and pushed herself as high as she could until she was almost on his shoulders, reaching with her finger tips for the little package. Just as she grasped it she felt Robert stumble. They fell to the floor in a heap.

Alice heard the whispering singers again and the Indian drum began to beat. She started to feel sick.

"Do you feel weird?" she said.

"Oh yes!" said Robert. "Here we go! Whatever's in that packet must be a Time Trigger. I think we're off on a time travelling quest!"

"I can feel evil all around us, Rob," said Alice. She felt dizzy and her heart thumped wildly. "I'm very afraid."

"We'll be O.K.," said Robert. "We always are."

The nausea in Alice's stomach was almost unbearable and she closed her eyes. Before she could say anything, she was surrounded by an explosion of purest white. They were time travelling. An arc of star dust spread out before her like the tail of a comet. She kept very still as she moved back across the dimensions of space and time.

A cool wind brushed her face.

"Oops. Trouble," said Robert.

Alice opened her eyes and stared at the pair of long leather boots on the grass close to their faces. Instinctively, her fingers tightened around the package.

"Hello," said a sneering voice.

Alice's heart was racing. Concealing the parcel against the side of her body, she brought herself onto her knees and bravely turned to look into the face of her attacker.

3

Friends and Enemies

The clouds parted. Moonbeams bounced from the metal foil quivering only centimetres from Robert's face. Alice had seen fencing equipment before but this was not a sporting sword. There was no protection from its sharp tip.

"Stand up!" said the man. With his other hand, he removed his hat. It had a buckled hat-band. His thin lips parted into a cruel smile. He was sturdily built with a square jaw and bushy eyebrows. There was dust on his worn leather doublet. "Come here, girl. Let me see you. I am supposed to kill you but you might fetch a good price with the savages. Profit would be even better. Either way, you would disappear!"

Robert stepped in front of Alice.

"Leave her alone," he said.

"Well, well," said the man. "I really can't be bothered to argue with infants. I've got better things to do. Pity. You look strong, Robert. With your special powers we could do so much. We could grow even richer and more powerful. But I can see from your eyes that you would be difficult hostages. Killing you will be much easier. Sir Ferdinando was right. But you are an insult really. After all those savages, he sends me to kill mere children! No matter. My blade will not need much cleaning."

"Are you going to murder us?" said Robert.

"Dispose of you," snarled the man.

"Why? What have we done?" said Robert.

"Nothing . . . yet," said the man. "It is what you

might do that must be prevented."

"What..."

"Shut up, boy!" snapped the man. "Time is short. Farewell!"

He drew back his arm.

"No...!" shouted Alice. She was about to leap at him when she heard a whistling sound in the darkness, followed by a thud.

The man's face contorted in pain and he made a strange snorting sound as he fell forwards. Alice jumped back to avoid his flailing sword. Blood trickled from a large gash on the back of his head. Robert and Alice peered into the darkness. Alice gasped as someone appeared from the shadows, someone whose appearance made her freeze with fear.

"It is you who are the savage," said a tall Indian. He spat on the unconscious man and kicked aside the rock that he had used to strike him. He looked up at Robert and Alice and his mask of hatred melted into a roguish grin.

His muscular chest was bare, save for three necklaces. He wore blue trousers and his plaited black hair was decorated with two feathers. Alice could see that he had shaved the sides of his head. He had an earring in one ear. His feet were covered in soft leather moccasins. Painted streaks of yellow and black decorated the olive skin on his face and chest and in one hand, he held a feathered axe.

"Sorry. Nearly missed all the fun, didn't I?" he laughed. "But better late than never!"

"Who are you?" said Robert.

"Call me Squanto," said the young man, picking up the sword. He bowed graciously. "Squanto of the Wampanoag Tribe. Time traveller and servant of the *Sachem* Massasoit, the greatest chieftain of my tribe. He is a powerful Time Regent. Chief Massasoit has sent me back to your cold and greedy land to get you out of trouble. That trouble." He prodded the other man with the sword. The man groaned.

"Who is he?" said Alice.

"That scumbag is Captain Hunt. Murdering dog of the evil Sir Ferdinando Gorges of the oh-so-prestigious Plymouth Company. This company draws up plans for my peoples' lands in the name of your King James."

Alice and Robert looked at Squanto in confusion.

"Oh. Forgive me. I do not blame you for the tyranny of your forebears. Sir Ferdinando Gorges was one of your powerful British knights who lay siege to my homeland with the blessing of your king. I suppose by now, in your time, these savage conquerors have been dead for so long that they are distant figures in your history. The annihilation of one race and the slavery of others in the quest for gold five hundred years ago is not your fault."

He squinted at Alice and Robert, running his fingers along the blade of the sword provocatively. Then he suddenly flicked into his clowning grin again.

"Enough of politics! You two have a mighty quest to save the lives of many. It is you who must bring medicine."

"What medicine?" said Alice.

"Bring it where?" said Robert.

Before Squanto could answer, the Captain groaned again and stirred.

"Umm. Now what shall I do with YOU? There is no pain great enough," said the young Indian. "Get up, scum!"

Captain Hunt rolled over in the dirt and sat up,

rubbing the back of his head.

"Up, I said!" Squanto pressed the tip of the sword into the man's cheek drawing a drop of blood.

"You won't succeed, savage," said the Captain.

"Oh? Since when has brute force been the conqueror of wisdom? Massasoit has taught me that," said Squanto.

"Since NOW!"

With a sudden sweep of both hands, Captain Hunt pulled out his muskets. Alice saw Squanto's flinch of annoyance as he threw down the sword.

"Come on now, Captain. We don't want to..." started Squanto.

"Shut up, savage!" shouted the other man, shuffling back against the church wall. He levered himself up against it, the muskets still pointing at the young Indian.

Alice glanced at Robert. He was glaring at her, nodding slightly in the direction of her pocket. She remembered the package. Inside was a Time Trigger. Maybe she could use it. But what about Robert? He wasn't touching her. He wouldn't be able to travel with her. And Squanto?

At that exact moment, another cool wind spiralled into the dirt of the churchyard path. The dust flurry cleared from the shimmering Time Tunnel and a tall man emerged.

"Dear, oh dear, Squanto my old friend," said the newcomer. "You are losing your touch!"

Alice recognised him immediately. He was the American time traveller from Gainsborough Hall. He had discarded the puritan collar now and was pointing a gun at Captain Hunt.

"Ethan!" said Squanto. "Good timing, my friend!" He rolled the whites of his eyes, grinning sarcastically and juggling the handle of his axe like a cheerleader's baton. He looked back at Captain Hunt. "Oops! Now the bully is outnumbered. Will he surrender? If not, which one of us will he shoot? Um, I wonder now? Me or thee, Ethan?"

Captain Hunt snarled like a wild animal. He threw his guns onto the floor. The tall American kicked them away.

"Look out!" yelled Alice, seeing the flick of the Captain's wrist. Before Squanto or Ethan could stop him, Captain Hunt released the dagger. It flew across the graveyard. Squanto whooped loudly. Another silver streak flashed in the moonlight. Metal struck metal in a fountain of sparks.

It was Alice who yelled. She stumbled and fell, screaming in pain. The Captain's deflected dagger had struck her. Robert rushed to her side.

"My arm!" shouted Alice.

Squanto and the tall American lunged towards the Captain, thrusting him against the church wall.

"Oh, no you don't," said Ethan, pulling a short leather strap from his belt. He tied Captain Hunt's arms together behind his back.

Squanto squatted beside Alice. He tore back the sleeve of her blazer.

"The wound is not deep. This jacket is thick," he said.

"Thank goodness," said Robert.

Squanto ripped off the remainder of the sleeve. He turned it inside out and folded it against the oozing wound. Alice moaned.

"Keep pressing on here, Alice," said Squanto. "You may need to bring the edges of the wound together with needle and thread."

"Stitches?" said Robert.

"Yes. I do not have my own needle here with me. Do you not have a *powachee* . . . a medicine man . . . in your village, who could mend Alice?" said Squanto.

"A doctor could," said Robert.

"Sure. If that is what you call your healers," said Squanto.

"I'm O.K.," said Alice, struggling to her feet.

"That wound will need cleaning soon, to prevent poison spreading. But there is no great urgency," said Ethan. "Squanto, I shall take our unpleasant friend for a long walk, while you show our new associates inside to meet Will."

"Excuse me," called Alice, as the American started to march his captive in the direction of the gate. "This is the second time we have met. Who are you and why are you helping us?"

"Oh, pardon me, Ma'am," said the tall young man in his American accent. He swept off his wide brimmed hat and brushed it across his breeches in a regal bow. "Ethan Allen at your service. Time Regent and sometime philosopher, soldier and revolutionary, lately travelled here from my own time in the eighteenth century by means of the Time Tunnel you just saw. I trust you enjoyed my little game back in Gainsborough on the stage with the players? I couldn't resist! For this quest, I am called to work once more with my ol' travelling partner from the seventeenth century, young Squanto here. It is a very great honour, brother."

He bowed again, this time at Squanto and walked away, pushing a scowling Captain Hunt in front of him.

Squanto nodded and grinned.

"Who's Will?" said Robert.

"Come on," said Squanto. "I will introduce you to William Bradford."

4

The Indian Arrowhead

"Which century are we in now?" said Alice, trying not to wince. Her arm was throbbing now.

"Mine," said Squanto. "This quest is in my time. The year is 1619. I have visited Ethan's century many times and witnessed the American fight for independence from the British in the 1770's and Ethan's own struggle to keep his beloved Vermont from being swallowed into the United States. This time, the tables are turned. It is I who needs Ethan's help, for my quest and yours will take us into Ethan's mountainous frontierland."

"I knew it!" said Robert. "I'm going snowboarding to Vermont next week. That's why you've come, isn't it? We have to help you over there in America, once we get there."

"Not me, then," said Alice. "I'm not going skiing with you. Your cousin is."

Robert screwed up his face in disgust.

"Jessica's not a Time Traveller. She can't help. Besides, I want you..."

Robert stopped. Alice noticed he was blushing slightly.

"Are you feeling strong, Alice?" said Squanto.

She nodded.

"Then let's go inside the church, friends," said Squanto.

"Just a minute," said Alice. "What's inside this package?"

"Oh. You haven't opened it?" said Squanto.

"No. There wasn't time before Captain Hunt attacked us," said Alice. "Whatever it is worked as a Time Trigger the moment I picked the package up. It must be very powerful."

Squanto raised one eyebrow and smiled knowingly.

"Naturally. It was crafted by my forefathers many thousands of years ago, after the glacial passage closed through which they had crossed into the new world from the old."

"What glacial passage?" said Alice.

"The frozen walkway called the Bering Straits that once connected what you call Alaska with Asia. That land bridge has long since disappeared under water but it is how the first of my people entered the continent long ago."

"I thought Indians were native Americans," said Robert.

Squanto rolled his eyes and started to giggle. Then he roared with laughter.

"I can see the great Sachem Massasoit has a great deal to teach you," he spluttered. "Do you even know from where such names as *Indian* and *America* derive?" Robert shook his head and Alice shrugged.

"I thought not. I have much to show you, English friends. But now, open the pouch."

Alice tried to pull the cord to open the soft pouch.

"I can't do this with one hand," she said, passing it to Robert.

He unwrapped it gently.

"There's something bony and hard inside," said Robert. "And there's another layer. This is like playing 'pass-the-parcel'."

Robert lifted the flaps of the second wrapping. In his hand he held the tip of an arrow.

"This arrowhead is a powerful Time Trigger," said

Squanto. "And here is another."

From an amulet around his neck, Squanto plucked a small stone.

"This is a Spirit Pond rune stone," he said. "For you."

He held it out to Robert.

"Cool," said Robert, examining the strange markings on the ancient stone. "What is it?"

"There are many of these in the safekeeping of our elders. They were left by early white men. Some of their tribes had wise sachems called druids who could also talk with the spirits, who, all those centuries ago, foretold of a far greater invasion of Europeans."

"What early white men?" said Alice. "I thought it was the pilgrims who discovered America."

Squanto shook his head.

"*Discovered* America? It did not need discovering!" he said, grinning again. "Sorry. I must not laugh at your ignorance. No. The visiting whitemen I mean were Norsemen."

"Vikings?" said Alice and Robert together.

"Of course. The Norsemen reached the shores of my continent just as they reached the shores of England. Some of them stayed and joined our tribes. Their medicine men brought new wisdom that enriched our healers in their own journeys with the spirits. They left many markings. Not all of their stones have magic but this one has helped Massasoit to see into the future and what must be done. He said to give it to you."

"I'll keep it safe," said Robert.

"Before you do," said Squanto. "I must ask you to return it and also the arrowhead while we are in the church. Ordinary mortals cannot see time travellers who are out of their own time while they hold Time

Triggers, remember?"

Alice and Robert nodded.

"It is important that our guest in there can see you. He is not a time traveller but he needs your help. I will look after the Triggers, as I have been doing up till now, and I will return them when we depart."

Robert hesitated. Squanto smiled at him.

"You are right to be suspicious, friend," he said. "You should trust no-one. But I give you my solemn oath on the lives of my people that all our destinies are entwined in this quest. I am not a Regent who has turned towards the forces of evil. I am your brother, friend and guide on this quest. Ethan and I have been guardians of these Triggers while we awaited your arrival. Look into my soul and see if you believe me."

Alice stared into Squanto's dark eyes and felt the pull of mighty forces. A shiver coursed through her like hot metal. She blinked and looked at Robert.

"Well?" said Robert. "What should I do? Your instincts have never been wrong, Alice."

"Give them to him," said Alice. Squanto's smiling eyes greeted her like glowing amber.

Robert wrapped the arrowhead in its leather pouch and passed the two Time Triggers back to the young man.

"The quest is at hand," said Squanto, turning. "Follow me."

He turned the heavy iron door handle and pushed. The door creaked open. Alice wrinkled up her nose at the musty smell of candle wax as Squanto led them down the side of the pews in the gloomy light. The door slammed shut behind them.

There was no sign of anybody. The pews were empty. Alice looked around her in the dim light.

Then she saw a face. It was grotesque and haunting. She stifled a cry and nudged Robert.

"Umm. Handsome fellow," whispered Robert, as they walked past the ancient gargoyle. Alice shuddered and tried not to look at it. Squanto stopped. He was listening. He turned his head from side to side like a bird. Then he winked at Alice and Robert and without warning, he danced behind a pillar, silent in his moccasins. Then he sprang around to the other side with a low whoop.

"Argh!" cried a young man, stepping back from the shadows. He was dressed in the white collar and dark suit of a puritan. Alice thought he looked about the same age as Squanto.

"Stop messing about," he said, looking annoyed.

Squanto followed him out from behind the pillar, sniggering. The young man jumped as he noticed Alice and Robert for the first time.

"So...Squanto has found you as he promised. Good. The Lord is indeed merciful. Well done friend."

He walked towards Robert and offered him his hand in friendship.

"Good evening," he said. "My name is William Bradford."

He removed his hat and bowed to Alice. His face was handsome but weary.

"Are you the William Bradford who will take the Pilgrim Fathers to America and become their leader?" said Alice, smiling.

William looked slightly confused. He turned to Squanto who shrugged.

"I have not heard this name Pilgrim Fathers," said William. "But I am soon to sail to the New World with a bold and desperate group of fellow Separatists. It is too dangerous in England. The king fears us, and his men try to silence us. We have been in exile in Holland and have returned to England to sail on the *Mayflower*. My friends are in hiding from the king's men near Plymouth, awaiting the ship's departure. I have returned to the church where I first found hope, in order to meet with you. Perhaps it is indeed God's will that I should one day lead my people in our new land. But for now I have been summoned here."

"Who summoned you?" said Robert.

"I had a vision," said William. "In it I was told I would meet a native from the New World, a praying Indian, who would warn me of a terrible danger that awaits my people. Then I met Squanto. He had allowed himself to be captured by the evil men who seek gold in the New World in the name of the king. He learned our language and escaped to find me and tell me I must come here to meet with you. Only you two have the power to save both our peoples."

5

Retreat

"I think you had a vision from the Spirits of Time," said Robert.

William Bradford looked at him blankly. Squanto stepped forwards.

"William has never travelled the pathways of time as you and I have done," he said quickly. "He does not have the powers. But my sachem, my wise chief, the great Massasoit, has explained that there are mortals who must be granted partial sight of the other dimensions in order to fulfill the spirits' prophesies and benefit quests. Some, like William, must be allowed to see us and know something of our mission."

"Like King William the Conqueror did, on one of our other quests? He could not time travel, but he did meet us and he saw inside Time Tunnels," said Alice.

"I expect so," said Squanto.

"I do not understand the magic of the people of the New World," interrupted William Bradford. "But I know that it is God's will that I should flee across the ocean with my people. In the New World we may die, but we shall endeavour to find a free land where we can practice our religion away from persecution and corruption. We seek only peace with the natives. They have been kind to early settlers, despite what Sir Ferdinando Gorges and his captains would like us to believe. Gorges wants to find the Golden City and bring its treasures here to England. That is not the way of Separatists, or of God. We seek only peace."

"What golden city?" said Robert, his eyes gleaming.

"Gorges believes in the legend of Norumbega," said Squanto. "White men have told of such a place. It is supposed to be a city belonging to my people that is filled with gold and wine."

"Where is it?" said Robert, looking very interested.

Squanto roared with laughter.

"Enough of this!" he shouted. "It has no bearing on our quest."

Robert opened his mouth to speak.

"Be quiet, Robert," said Alice. "I don't like that greedy look in your eyes. Let William tell us what we must do."

Robert scowled and gestured for William to continue.

"So why do you need our help?" said Alice to William.

"Squanto has told of the great plague that lurks in the New World, brought across on the ships of the explorers. It will spread to his people and mine. It will kill me first," said William Bradford. "His chief, called Massasoit, whom I am very keen to meet, has seen that you two have powerful medicine that will save us."

"Massasoit says that great peace talks will be made. But only with those white men and women and the people of the great tribes who bring peace in their hearts, instead of guns in their belts," said Squanto. "These talks will be the beginning of a new, free nation. But the plague will prevent such treaties."

"Gorges would like to see us die," said William.

"Why?" said Alice.

"Because our beliefs are a threat to the power of

the king because we worship God directly, not through the king's bishops who we do not acknowledge as our masters. That is still a threat for the king even if we escape across the ocean to his colonies. And any threat to the king is a threat to Gorges' power. And if we pilgrims are at peace with the natives, Gorges' imperial plans in the name of the king are at risk," said William.

"Plus he'd like to take all my people as slaves for his plantations and his quest for gold," said Squanto. "The spirits of evil champion his tyranny and warn him. He knows that if your quest succeeds, your medicine will save the people who oppose him and the treaty will be signed. The spirits of evil have no doubt let him see into the future pathways of time. He will try to stop you, Alice and Robert."

"You two have the power to keep the timeline true," said William.

"William Bradford must not die, my friends," said Squanto. "The destiny of a nation is in your hands. You have the medicine."

"What medicine?" said Alice.

"If you do not yet know that, it will be shown to you," said Squanto. His dark eyes shone. "Ethan and I will protect you until the spirits guide you. Massasoit will help us. It is also my private hope that you can somehow save my people from destruction at the hands of those, like Gorges, who seek to steal our lands. But that is probably a silly dream."

"That *would* change the course of history," said Robert.

"I know," said Squanto. "And maybe it is not the will of the spirits. Massasoit says that the need to conquer is the curse of all mankind anyway. So if one race did not succeed, another would come along to try."

"I'd like to have a go at finding the golden city of Norumbega," said Robert.

Alice glanced at him. There was something dark and dangerous in his eyes.

"I wouldn't," she said. "But I would very much like to meet your wise chief...your *sachem*...if that's the right word?" said Alice.

Squanto smiled at her.

"Yes, powerful white woman. You speak my tongue with a good accent. I hope I will have time to teach you more."

Alice nodded eagerly.

"My friends, there will be much bloodshed," said Squanto. "For I have seen how the sachem shakes and sweats when he has visions and communes with the spirits. Dark shadows may yet envelop us. But Massasoit says that you two must first bring the medicine."

"Do you think that Robert and I are both going to America?" said Alice.

Squanto nodded.

"But I'm not..."

Before Alice could finish, the church door burst open. William tensed and Squanto lifted his axe. It was Ethan.

"We have to go, my friends," he panted, sprinting up the aisle. Sweat was running down his face. Alice could see fresh blood on his jacket. "Captain Hunt must have alerted his men before he came. I held them off as long as I could before running to warn you. Squanto, take Mr Bradford to safety...quickly! The rest of us must time travel. Now! We cannot wait. They will be here any minute."

Squanto reached into his amulet and passed Alice

the Time Triggers. She caught a fleeting smile as he touched her hand.

"Go!" he shouted, pulling William towards a side door. "Don't worry about us. I have horses hidden at the back of the church. We will be safe."

Alice passed the Spirit Pond rune stone back to Robert.

"Will we see you again, Ethan?" said Robert, taking Alice's other hand.

"Oh, yes!" smirked Ethan. "We have only just begun. Farewell, friends!"

He ducked down and touched the floor of the church drawing an arc over his head. The air around him started to flicker in a haze. Alice knew it was a Time Tunnel. She gripped Robert's hand and the arrowhead packet.

Suddenly, the church door flew open. Captain Hunt sprang to face them, aiming his muskets.

Alice closed her eyes and concentrated her thoughts on travelling back to her own time. She heard a distant bang and the acid scent of gunpowder traced through the air as she time travelled. She had escaped the musket shot just in time. Then she had a terrifying thought. Captain Hunt could see her earlier when she was holding the arrowhead, so he was a time traveller. What if he was one of the all-powerful Time Regents who could generate Time Tunnels even without a Trigger? Gigantic eddies of colour flashed around her senses. She felt a bump and opened her eyes. All around her was blackness.

She gripped Robert's hand.

"We're still in the church, aren't we?" she whispered.

"I think so," said Robert. He stood up.

"At least we're alone," said Alice.

"You think that's a good thing?" said Robert.
Alice felt Robert shiver.
"Yes. I don't like the dark, but it's better than Captain Hunt and his guns," she said.
"My eyes are focusing a bit, now," said Robert.
Just then, the moon came out and beams of silver light glinted through the windows, turning into arcs of purple and red where the panes were stained glass.
"Oh, that's better," said Alice. She grasped the wooden lectern to pull herself up. Her fingers felt the smooth contours of a small carving on the base.
"Oh! What's this?" she said. "It's a cute little wooden mouse. How clever!"
"There's another one here," said Robert, examining the choir stalls. "And another. I wonder how many the carpenter has hidden?"
"We'll have to come back some day. No time to play around just at the moment," said Alice. "Pity. Look at that wonderful model of a ship."
"It's the *Mayflower*," said Robert, squinting to read the label on the glass cabinet in the moonlight. "I think it's made out of thousands of match sticks. Incredible!"
"The gargoyles are still here," said Alice. She stuck her tongue out at the stony features of the jug-eared imp. "It's worn away in places now, but I bet William Bradford would still recognise it."
They walked across to the door, over the ornate iron grid that ran between the relatively modern Victorian floor tiles. Robert turned the door handle. Nothing happened.
"Oh, no! It's locked," he said, rattling the huge mortise lock.
They turned back and looked around.
"The side door," they said together, grinning.

Robert skidded down the aisle and swept back a modern curtain.

"Phew!" he said. "It's still here."

He tugged on the dusty bolt. For a moment, nothing happened. Then it gave way and Robert fell back against Alice. Her injured arm squashed against a pillar.

"Ow!" she moaned.

The blazer dressing fell off. The wound was still oozing. It looked very dirty. Alice winced at the congealed mess that stuck to her skin.

"I'm gonna have to get that seen to," she muttered. "I'll have to tell Mr Picket I fell. I don't want him to get into trouble for letting us come here."

Robert turned the iron loop of the handle and the little door began to open.

"If I stay close to you, he might not see your torn sleeve in the dark," said Robert. "But you must find some excuse to tell your Mum when we get home. It needs cleaning. Maybe you need to make an appointment with your doctor."

"We'll see," said Alice. "Stay close."

They slipped out of the church and found their way between the graves. Mr Picket was waiting for them at the gate.

"Ah, ha! There you are," said the teacher. "You look a bit shifty, the pair of you. What have you been up to?"

"Reading inscriptions on the grave stones, Sir," said Alice.

"In the dark?" said Mr Picket.

"I've got a torch," said Robert innocently.

"Umm," said Mr Picket. He looked satisfied with their story. "Great place, this. You can positively *feel* the history. Probably dozens of ghosts here. Very inspiring. Shame we've got to go, but I think

I've left those heathens on the bus long enough. Time we were off."

"He's cool," whispered Robert to Alice as they walked back down the drive.

Alice nodded and smiled. She turned to look over her shoulder at the silhouette of Babworth church skulking between the trees.

"We need to talk," she said to Robert. "Urgently."

6

Doctor Sedall

Robert sat close to Alice.

"Does your arm still hurt?" he asked.

"Uh, huh," said Alice.

She squinted down at the wound. It was red and dirty.

"I'll clean it up when I get back to my house," she said. Alice turned to Robert. "Rob?"

"Yes?"

"You know that golden city... Norumbega or something...?"

"Ye-es?" Robert's eyes darted with interest.

"Well, you wouldn't really go and look for it when you go to America, would you?"

"Maybe," said Robert. "Why not?" he continued. "Surely you'd like to find it too?"

Alice looked at him in surprise.

"I'm not sure. I don't think it has anything to do with us."

Robert turned away and looked out of the window.

"We each have our own destiny," he said quietly.

Alice felt uneasy. She sat back in her seat until they got back to school.

At home, Alice raced up to the bathroom. She washed her arm in the sink with soapy water and dabbed it dry with a clean towel. It throbbed more, but it looked better. She rummaged through the chest in the bathroom and found a crépe bandage still in its wrapper. She did her best with one hand but it wasn't easy. She wound it over and over, on top of the wound. Then, she pushed the torn blazer to the bottom of her wardrobe and searched through her hangars until she found her old blazer. It was very tight these days and the sleeves were too short, but if she skipped wearing her school jumper tomorrow, and wore her black coat on top on the way to school, nobody would notice the difference.

The next day was Thursday. It was a cold December morning and grey clouds hung low in the sky threatening snow. Alice rushed into school to find Robert. She wanted to talk more about the quest and help Robert plan what to do once he was over in America at the weekend. Robert saw Alice first.

"Hey!" he shouted at her across the playground. He was grinning excitedly as he ducked between the other pupils. "It's a miracle!"

Alice frowned at him.

"Explain," she said, as Robert panted to catch his breath.

"She can't come," puffed Robert. "Jessica. My cousin. She's twisted her ankle ice-skating. She can't come to America!"

Alice's mind started to race.

"So..." Robert winked at Alice. "I asked if you could come instead. And..."

"And what?" said Alice.

"They said yes. Mum and Dad don't mind, if your parents are O.K. about it. They should be able to swap the tickets with the airline. Isn't it amazing?" said Robert.

"Yes," said Alice, fumbling in her bag for her mobile phone. "I'll ring Mum now. There will be things to sort out. I hope there's enough time."

"There should be. Grown-ups travel at short notice, on business and things, don't they?"

"Yeah. Just a sec... Mum? It's me, Mum. I need to

ask you something really exciting..."

Alice's Mum said she'd ring Robert's parents. Alice was too excited to concentrate on her lessons all morning. Even drama. She switched her phone back on at lunchtime. There was a text message waiting.

"YES!" she shouted, punching the air.

She ran outside to find Robert.

"Mum's cool!" she said when she found him. "She's spoken to your Mum and they're making all the arrangements. You're going to pick me up at seven o'clock on Saturday morning. Mum even said she'd wash my ski gear from last year. Hope it still fits. I've never been to America, Rob. This is amazing!"

Alice heard even less of what her teachers were saying in the afternoon. She spent most of the French lesson writing lists of what she needed to pack when she got home. During maths, she drew lots of bubbles on the back page of her rough book and wrote a clue to the quest in each one. She drew lines in between the clue bubbles that seemed to be linked. There were lots of question marks.

That evening, she re-packed her case three times. It was really difficult to get everything in. The salopettes were really bulky. Her moon boots were too small now, which was just as well as there wasn't enough room for them anyway.

She reached under her pillow and pulled out the small bundle hidden beneath. She patted it gently.

"This must stay in my hand luggage," she whispered. "No! On second thoughts, in my pocket!" She smiled to herself. "Ow!" The wound on her arm throbbed as she knocked it on the side of the bed. She took off the baggy bandage. With a sigh, she went downstairs to show her mother.

"Oh, Alice!" said her mother. "How long have you had this?"

"This morning," said Alice. "I fell off the bus."

"Good grief! Poor you," said Mrs Hemstock. "I don't like the look of that, Alice. I'm going to ring the doctor's surgery first thing in the morning. Hopefully the nurse will be able to look at it. Let's put a clean dressing on it overnight. Come on. Upstairs. Does it hurt?"

"Only a bit," said Alice. She didn't want to sound in too much pain in case her mum said she couldn't go to America.

It wasn't too painful in the morning but Alice's mum insisted on ringing the surgery. Luckily there was a cancellation, so at ten o'clock Alice found herself sitting with her mother in the busy conservatory waiting room. She suddenly had the feeling that she was being watched.

Alice looked around the room again. If any of these people were time travellers, would she know?

A young woman emerged from the room with a seven on the door. She was carrying a piece of paper. She smiled to herself until she noticed Alice staring at her and quickly put the paper away in her handbag on her way out. Alice was just wondering what the paper could say when she heard her name over the crackly speaker. Her mother put down the magazine she was reading and they knocked on the door of number seven.

Doctor Sedall looked up from the computer screen and swivelled on his chair. He looked at Alice over the rims of his half-moon glasses. His eyes glinted under his high forehead as he nodded at Alice's mum and beckoned Alice to sit on the chair at the side of the desk.

"Now then, young lady," he said. He had an

American accent. "What can I do for you today?"

"I've hurt my arm," said Alice. "I fell over. Yesterday."

"Let's take a look shall we?" said Doctor Sedall.

Alice pulled her arm out of her cardigan sleeve and gently peeled back the dressing.

"Umm," said the doctor. "Nasty. What did you say you cut it on?"

"The ground," said Alice, looking straight at the doctor.

He frowned.

"That's a very straight edge. Are you sure you haven't run into any knives or swords lately?"

Alice heard her mum draw breath. Alice shook her head and said nothing.

"Umm," said the doctor again, pausing to look at Alice suspiciously.

"Is she up to date with her tetanus, Mrs Hemstock?" said the doctor.

"Oh, yes," said Alice's mum. "Is it serious?"

"Well, ideally, it should have had a few stitches. But it looks as if the wound is healing very quickly. Remarkably quickly. It could be infected though. Especially if anything old or rusty caused it." He stared at Alice for a moment.

"Alice is supposed to be going on holiday to America tomorrow," said her mum. "Will it still be all right for her to travel?"

"A traveller, eh?" said the doctor, looking at Alice over his glasses again. "I can't see why not. I think it might be wise to take some antibiotics with you though. Are you allergic to anything?"

Alice shook her head.

The doctor turned away to the computer screen. He tapped the prescription onto the keyboard and pressed the print button.

"These should do the trick," he said. "One, four times a day."

"Do I have to take them?" said Alice.

"I would strongly recommend it," said Doctor Sedall. "Take them with you. But don't let them fall into the wrong hands, will you?"

Alice stared at the doctor. He looked directly back. A reflection from the room light danced briefly in his steadfast eyes. Alice swallowed. She took the prescription and folded it in half. Then she put it in her pocket. Was Doctor Sedall a Time Regent? Had he blended into the community, waiting for the chance to help Alice on her quest, as other Time Regents had done before?

"Now, pop across to the nurse and she'll give you a supply of clean dressings," said the doctor. "There. My job is done. But yours is just beginning, Alice. Take care abroad, won't you?"

Alice frowned at the doctor.

He stood up signalling the end of the consultation.

"Is it hard to be a doctor?" said Alice.

"Why? Do you want to be a healer, Alice?" he said.

"Maybe. I was wondering how I would know if you were just acting."

"Alice!" said her mother.

"A fair question, young lady. You mean how do you know if I'm prescribing you poison?"

Alice nodded slowly.

"Do I look like an imposter?"

Alice studied the man's face. His dark eyes shone brightly. She felt a shiver of power inside.

"No."

The tall man smiled.

"Come on, Alice," said Mrs Hemstock. "Thank you, doctor."

"Grab your destiny, Alice," said the doctor. "Do

what you enjoy and what you believe to be right and you will succeed."

"Are you an American *Regent*?" said Alice impulsively.

Doctor Sedall winked at her.

"I am originally from America and my greatest hobby is travelling. Does that answer your question?" he said.

Alice nodded.

"Really, Alice!" said her mum. "I'm sure the doctor is a very busy man."

"It's quite all right, Mrs Hemstock," said Doctor Sedall.

"Could I be a ... like you one day?" said Alice.

"Of course. You can be anything you want to be. You could be a doctor and go on quests with a lot of travelling. Do you like solving mysteries?"

"Oh, yes," said Alice.

"Well, diagnosis is a kind of quest. It's like collecting clues in a detective mystery," said the doctor. "Or doing a jig-saw puzzle. But you do need all the pieces."

Alice smiled at him. She felt sure he was a Time Regent in disguise, but one who was working for the quest, not one who had turned to work for the forces of evil. Probably.

"Thank you," she said.

He nodded.

"Oh, Alice," he called after her. "I almost forgot. Take this. I don't need it any more." He passed her a pocket-sized medical manual. "If I come across strange symptoms, I look them up in a book. Remember that. Goodbye."

Alice looked at the book.

"Thank you," she said. "I'll look after this."

"That's very kind, doctor," said Mrs Hemstock.

"Just doing my job," said Dr Sedall.

Alice saw his wink as her mother closed the door. She looked at the gap under the door in case she caught a glimpse of any flashes of white light. But the tannoy crackled into life summoning a restless young man with a breathing problem into room seven. She put the little textbook into her pocket.

"How long has Dr Sedall been here?" asked Alice as the nurse dressed her wound.

"He's a locum," said the nurse.

"A what?"

"A locum is like a supply teacher at school. Someone who comes in at short notice when someone is ill. I've never met Dr Sedall before. He's new. From the agency."

Alice's heartbeat quickened with excitement.

7

America

Alice hugged her mother at the customs barrier.

"Now you have got everything, haven't you?" said Mrs Hemstock. "Your passport?"

"Yes, Mum."

"Ski socks?"

"Yes."

"Sun cream?"

"Yes."

"Medicine for your arm?"

"Oh yes. Definitely that, Mum. Just in case of emergency. Please don't worry so much! But the wound on my arm is almost healed. Almost like magic, really. I don't think I'm going to need the tablets."

Alice had told Robert about Doctor Sedall. They both agreed that he was a Time Regent. Alice had examined the tablets suspiciously but they were boring, white, powdery things that probably tasted disgusting.

They boarded the aeroplane. It was huge inside. A great big jumbo.

"It's got an upstairs!" said Alice.

"For very posh people," said Robert.

"Our seats do have their own telly screens on the back of the chair in front. Look!" said Alice.

They investigated the contents of the seat pocket and found ear phones, socks, a mask to block out the daylight if you fancied a snooze and a long list of all the different movies and games you could play on the twenty-five channels.

"Wow! Cool or what?" said Robert, settling into his seat between Alice and his dad.

It was a great flight. Seven hours of films, computer games and free drinks.

"Boston is six hours behind UK time," said Mr Davenport as they fastened their seat belts for the landing. "Better re-set your watches."

"I'll do your watch for you," said Robert. "If you want to close your eyes!"

"I'm much better on planes these days," said Alice. But she closed her eyes anyway, until she knew they were on the ground and slowing down.

The Davenports and Alice had to wait in a long queue at the immigration checkpoint.

"I feel like a criminal," huffed Mrs Davenport. She flicked her hair behind the padded shoulders of her fur coat, opened her handbag and took out a mirror to examine her make up.

Mr Davenport was filling in a long form with lots of questions. They shuffled round the snaking queue in between the ropes behind another family. The children, younger than Robert and Alice, wore ski jackets too. The little girl kept sticking her tongue out at Robert over her mother's shoulder.

"God! I hope they're not going to the same place as us," said Robert.

When they got to the front of the queue, they were interrogated about the purpose of their visit by a fat security officer. He spoke with an American accent. Alice was fascinated. She'd seen dozens of American programmes and films but this was the first time she had heard a real American speaking in real, live America.

"I'm really here," she whispered to herself.

"I heard that," said Robert, smiling. "The New World, eh? Do you feel the thrill too? Like we might find the secret city full of treasure?"

"I feel something. It's probably jet lag!" said Alice. She smiled at the gruff security man but he gave her a stony-faced stare. At last, he seemed satisfied and he dismissed them with a wave. They walked through into the arrivals hall, looking for the tour guide to show them to their coach.

Alice suddenly felt a shadow of fear shoot across her. She glanced behind. Two men were now at the security counter. She couldn't see their faces but she felt sure one of them had just turned back from looking at her. She shuddered.

"Over there, Michael," said Mrs Davenport to her husband. "That man is holding up a board with our name on."

"Well, hello there, Ma'am," bellowed the man. "Gee. I hope you all had a real nice trip."

"Not too bad, thank you," said Mr Davenport.

"Cramped," moaned Mrs Felicity Davenport. "But adequate. We need to get to our hotel. Is it far?"

"It should take us just about three hours to get up to Stowe on the freeway, Ma'am," said the man. He adjusted his baseball cap.

"THREE HOURS!" said Mrs Davenport.

"Yep." The man looked upset.

"My wife is very tired," said Mr Davenport. "Is there anyone else going to Stowe with us?"

"Nope. Not tonight. Your travel company hired me an' my truck to drive you all back over the mountains."

"No coach?" said Mrs Davenport.

"My chevvy is real comfy, Ma'am," said the man. "The name's Bob, by the way."

"Pleased to meet you, Bob," said Robert. He shook the man's hand. "Great name. I'm Rob."

"Pleased to meet you, Rob," said Bob, grinning. "I

plan to stop midway, at the liquor store. There's rest rooms there."

Robert's eyebrows shot up.

"Liquor sounds good," he joked.

"Not for you, young fella," said the driver, leading them towards the exit. "You can't drink liquor until you're twenny-one in the US. But your Mom or Pop might wanna buy a bottle or two while it's tax free. It'll cost you more once we cross the state boundary into Vermont."

They walked though the doors. The cold air greeted them like a wall of ice.

"Wow!" said Alice. "That's cold!"

"Yep. It'll probably drop to about ten below here in Boston. But it'll be more like thirty below up in the mountains. A real cold snap. Them arctic winds sure are chilly. Better keep them hats and mitts out!"

Bob walked off to fetch the chevvy. Again, Alice felt a wave of unease brush through her. She looked up and down in front of the terminal building. There was no sign of the two men.

Bob pulled up with the truck. He put their luggage in the back and covered it over. Alice and Robert climbed into the back seat. Mr and Mrs Davenport sat at the front on the bench seat next to Bob.

"All set then?" he said cheerfully, rubbing his hands together after slamming the truck door.

It was warm and comfy inside the truck. Alice wiped a patch in the condensation on her window and peered through the port hole, as the truck moved off into the streams of big American cars. One of the two men Alice had seen behind them at the security counter was emerging through the sliding doors. He threw his case onto the back seat of another truck with darkened windows. The second man got out from the driver's seat to scrape snow from the windscreen. He looked up at Alice. She couldn't see his face beneath his hat, but to her surprise, he waved menacingly. The next moment, he was lost to her view, as the traffic swept them onwards into the Boston night and out towards the freeway that would take them into Vermont. Alice sat back round suddenly.

"Hunt!" she said to Robert under her breath. "I think that might have been Captain Hunt!"

8

The Liquor Store

Robert looked at Alice and frowned, glancing over his shoulder into the night.

"You've seen Captain Hunt?" he said quietly.

"I don't know. I'm not sure. Whoever it was got into a car with another man."

"It could have been anyone," said Robert, yawning.

"Or it could have been time travelling spies keeping an eye on us," said Alice.

The chevvy purred along into the state of New Hampshire along the interstate highway, leaving behind the bright city lights of Boston, Massachusetts. Alice kept wiping her porthole in the condensation. The window glass was icy. When her hand got too cold, she took off her boot, leant back and started using her foot.

"Ha! Did you see that road sign?" she said. "It said *Grantham*. That's the same as the town near our Newark, at home in England."

"I saw *Norwich* and *Peterborough* on the map of America too," said Robert. "And places in Essex, England, where your Nan lives. There are loads of Newarks in America, you know! But we live in the real one of course... the very first one. The one that gets its name from the 'new work' the Saxons had to do to keep out the Vikings. Remember what Lady Godiva told us once?"

"Yes. I do. It's weird, isn't it?" said Alice. "Here we are, thousands of miles across the world and everywhere has familiar names."

"I suppose it must be the same for the Americans when they come to England," said Robert. "Definitely weird though!" He yawned again.

Bob chattered on, telling them about the great skiing, where to buy the best breakfasts and trips to various sights they might fancy. Mrs Davenport's head nodded forwards from time to time. Robert was dozing too. His head was resting on Alice's shoulder and getting heavy. She pushed him gently off and backwards against the seat.

She glanced out of the back window. Through the misted pane she could see the white glare of headlights on the vehicle behind. The distance never varied. If Bob's chevvy slowed, the vehicle behind slowed. If Bob speeded up, the headlights behind caught up quickly and stayed there like menacing torch beams, splayed out by the irregularities of the condensation on the window. She tried not to think about it.

"There's a real interesting place in Burlington, all done out like Victorian. Real old and historical..." Bob droned on.

Alice started to drift off too. Although it was only early evening in America, it was well after midnight in English time. She would give the older buildings a miss if they went to the city, she thought dreamily. They didn't sound that old. Her house in England was Georgian anyway. But the shopping mall sounded good. Alice heard the faint sound of Indian drums again. They lulled her to sleep.

She woke with a start as the truck stopped.

"Time to stretch your legs," said Bob. "The rest room's round the back. They've got machines to buy candy, if you're hungry. The liquor store at the front might be worth a visit for Mom and Pop there."

"Yes. I might..." started Mr Davenport.

"We don't need alcohol, Michael," snapped his wife. "We don't want to get drunk now, do we?"

Felicity Davenport minced off towards the toilets.

Bob opened the door for Alice and Robert. Flurries of snow swirled in their faces.

"Wicked!" said Robert, kicking at the packed snow that covered the car park. "Don't you need snow chains for driving, Bob?"

"Nah. Everyone here changes to winter tyres in the fall. Unless they're real stupid! Don't need no chains. Couldn't be takin' 'em on and off the whole time."

"What's the *fall*?" said Robert.

Bob looked at Robert in confusion. Then he laughed.

"Fall is the season in between summer and winter. You Brits call it autumn, don't you?"

"Oh. Thanks," said Robert.

"Do you want to buy a snack?" said Mr Davenport.

Alice and Robert nodded furiously.

"Here's some money, then," said Robert's dad, passing them each a small wadge of crisp green notes.

"Dollars!" smirked Robert, flicking the ends of the notes and looking shiftily at Alice. "Cool!"

The notes did feel good in Alice's hand, and they smelled terrific. She browsed along the machines.

"Oh, look... *Hershey* bars! I've seen them on *The Simpsons*. I'm going to try one," said Alice, pushing a dollar bill into the slot on the machine.

The chocolate dropped down.

"Candy bars for children!" hissed a voice.

Alice sprang round. Robert was nowhere to be seen.

"You!" she gasped.

Captain Hunt stood very close to her. He looked

more menacing than ever in his modern suit and dark sunglasses.

Instinctively, Alice felt for the arrowhead. It was safe in her pocket.

"Where's Robert?" she said suddenly.

"Gone back," sneered Hunt. "My friend Sir Ferdinando Gorges will take care of him. How's your arm?"

"Fine, thanks," said Alice. "What do you mean Robert's gone back?"

"With Gorges. To meet his destiny in our time," said Captain Hunt. "I think he liked us. A fine lad like Robert would make an excellent recruit for our cause. He's greedy for power. Sir Ferdinando is a very powerful master of time regency. A dark master, maybe, but one of the most powerful. He will easily persuade a weakling like Robert to realise that being in touch with your greedy side is being in control. But if you want to see him again ...alive...you'd better co-operate with me. No funny business with Triggers. Come on. Over here. We'll travel together."

Alice took a step backwards.

"Oh, don't be stupid, now," said Hunt. "If you don't come with me you'll never know where Robert has gone. It will be like trying to find a snail on a sandy beach."

Alice hesitated.

"I'll take you for a thrilling ride like no other... in a Time Tunnel. I can see you'd like to."

"You will kill me," said Alice.

Captain Hunt took off his glasses. His pupils glowed red in the centre of his black eyes.

"Not if you co-operate. We will take the Triggers and return you to your own lives. Unless you or Robert fancy joining forces with us."

"I will never cross over to your side!" said Alice. "And I'd be very surprised if Robert would."

"Never say never, Alice. Everyone has their price."

"That's not true!"

"Or you could always live with the savages," said Captain Hunt. "Maybe one day someone will ransom you. Then again, maybe not. Perhaps you wouldn't choose to be freed anyway. I have heard of silly young white girls taken hostage by the Indians who decide to stay in that primitive way of life. Looks like it might suit you too."

"Somehow, I'm not surprised people choose to live with the native people," said Alice. "If the alternative is life with the likes of you!"

She was beginning to feel cross. Anger gave her courage.

"You're the savages!" she shouted.

Captain Hunt's toad-like smile slipped. His lips curled wildly. Alice jumped as he moved. But he did not lunge towards her. Instead he crouched down and touched the floor. It sparked a brilliant light, stunning Alice.

He lifted his arm and stepped towards her. The light arced around them. Alice tried to step away, but her legs would not move. In a second, she was enveloped in a tunnel of light. Captain Hunt stretched his arms wide and gave a terrible howl. The light flashed between his hands like electricity and the ground shook.

Everything seemed to spin around and around in a massive attack of vertigo and nausea. But Alice did not fall. She tried to reach her pocket but the power in the tunnel was too strong. The white gave way to vivid spectral colours filling the space around her like a solar storm.

It stopped as quickly as it had started, releasing Alice with a jolt.

"Did you bring any of that liquor, Hunt?" said a crisp English voice. "We could always use it to weaken the natives."

Alice blinked and turned towards the voice.

"You must be Sir Ferdinando Gorges," she muttered.

The man nodded gracefully. He was tall and slender with shoulder length, dark wavy hair. He immediately reminded Alice of the salamanders she had seen in the reptile house at the zoo. His floppy cavalier hat was trimmed with ostrich feathers and his gathered breeches and tight fitting, embroidered doublet looked like costume from a Shakespeare play. His cuffs were trimmed with lace and his fine leather shoes were decorated with rosettes. He was flicking his gloves into the palm of one hand and his sleek moustache twitched menacingly.

Captain Hunt clicked the heels of his long, plain boots before tapping the ground with his walking stick and nodding at someone standing behind Alice.

Still stunned, Alice felt her arms being grabbed and thrust painfully behind her back. Her wrists were tied with a thin strap that cut into her flesh. She couldn't see her attacker.

Sir Ferdinando looked Alice up and down in approval.

"I think we should get a good price for this one," he said. He stroked his moustache and smiled at Alice.

"More like a fox," thought Alice. "And Hunt is the wolf."

Sir Ferdinando Gorges' face changed instantly into a mask of evil.

"Well, find the other Trigger, boy!" he growled.

Alice wriggled as she felt her captor searching her pockets.

"It's here," said the familiar voice.

"Throw it over to me," said Gorges.

"No!" shouted Alice.

But it was too late. The pouch with the arrowhead traced an arc above her head and landed deftly in the man's hand.

"Thank you. Now take her to my tent and get her ready. We will sell her when our guests arrive."

Alice's captor grabbed her by the arm. She winced as he squeezed her old knife wound. Then she gasped.

"It's you! My God! What have they done to you, Rob!" she screamed.

9

Wigwam

Robert's eyes were dark and threatening. He pushed Alice roughly towards the tent flap and out under the clear night sky.

"Rob! Wait! Stop . . ."

"Keep walking," he said.

"But . . . why?" said Alice. "Did they make you work for them? Have they given you drugs?"

"Shut up!" shouted Robert.

It was freezing outside. Without a coat, Alice started to shiver. The air was so cold it felt as though the hairs in her nostrils were icing up. The skin on her face was numb.

Robert pushed Alice across a snow-covered clearing. Tents were pitched all around. Men rushed between them from time to time. They approached a larger tent. Robert lifted the flap and pushed Alice inside. The air was warmer inside, heated by a fire.

"You're to go in there and change," said Robert, pointing to a cloth partition. The native girl will help you."

"But Rob . . ."

"In there!" he shouted, shoving her so hard she stumbled and almost fell.

Alice was close to tears. What had happened to Robert?

She ducked inside the inner tent. A Native American girl curtseyed slightly and took out a small knife. She saw the flicker of fear in Alice's face.

"Hands . . ." she said, motioning crossed, tied

hands and then the knife.

Alice understood that the girl would untie her. She turned slightly and held her bleeding wrists away from her back. The young woman cut the strap.

"Who are you?" said Alice, rubbing her wrists.

"Nobody," said the girl. Her eyes flickered with a note of warning.

"Nobody's *nobody*," said Alice. "Do you work for those Englishmen?"

The girl nodded. She had obviously been captive for some time and had learned some English. She pointed to the bed.

An elaborate outfit was laid out with a flat fronted, boned bodice trimmed with lace and pearls and a wide, hooped skirt with a petticoat.

"Is that for me?" said Alice. "How do you know it will fit?"

"Robert . . . " said the girl.

Alice moved to go back out to Robert. The Indian girl grabbed her arm.

"No! Dress . . . "

She shook her head and pointed back at the clothes.

"But I want to talk to my friend. I think he's in trouble," said Alice. "He wouldn't treat me like this, even if he did get tempted to be greedy. The forces of evil are hypnotising him. They are preying on his weakness."

"Not yet," said the girl. "You can help him after."

Alice was about to protest.

"Squanto says so," said the young woman suddenly.

Alice looked at her.

"Squanto knows I'm here?"

The girl's face relaxed into a slight smile and she

spoke more fluently in a hushed voice.

"Yes. He's coming to save you tonight. You must dress."

"And Robert? Is he going to rescue him too?"

The girl's face turned dark. She shook her head.

"I do not know if he can be saved," she said. "Robert has allowed himself to be turned towards the darkness. Robert works for Gorges now."

Alice looked back in the direction of the opening.

"Gold turns hearts," said the girl. "And Gorges has powerful evil spirits guiding him. Together, they can turn minds."

"Oh, Rob," murmured Alice. She was really worried about Robert now.

The girl looked at Alice and shrugged.

"Turn around," she said.

She laced the back of the bodice tightly. Alice had to concentrate to steady herself as the young woman tugged and pulled. The young Indian lifted the petticoat.

Alice sighed and said nothing. Her mind was racing. She was trying to think of a plan but she was distracted by the awkwardness of the clothing. The boned bodice was very stiff and the white ruff collar jabbed her chin if she looked down. She tried to keep still as the Native American girl fixed up her long hair.

"What's your name," said Alice.

"Call me Two Bears," said the girl, handing Alice a folded fan.

"You do not wear the English clothes," said Alice.

"Gorges likes me to dress as a squaw when other Indians are coming. It gives them trust, he thinks."

"Your tunic is very beautiful," said Alice, admiring the intricate beadwork on the soft leather. "Much nicer than these stuffy English clothes. Do you know Squanto? Are you from Squanto's tribe?"

"Squanto is my friend and I am in his tribe now. But he is Wampanoag. I am Abenaki originally. My people are from much farther north. But against Gorges and Hunt, we must be united. These English seek to turn us all to slavery to grow tobacco."

"Not all the English are bad, surely?" said Alice.

"No. Of course not. There is bad blood in every tribe and race. Some Europeans do come in peace to trade fur and fish."

"What about the pilgrims?"

"The ones who do not wear jewels and who pray?"

"Yes."

"There are not many of them. But more are coming. I do not yet know what this will mean. There. You are ready."

"For what?"

"Tonight, some of my people are invited by Gorges to eat and smoke with him."

"Is it a trick?"

"I'm not sure. I think Gorges wants to trade you for many native people who will work for him. Or for information. But Squanto says he has a plan."

"I hope so," said Alice.

Two Bears draped a cloak over Alice's shoulders and pointed to the curtain. Alice started to whisper.

"Will you be..."

But Two Bears put her finger to her lips and melted into the shadows,

Alice lifted the curtain flap and stepped back into the outer tent.

Robert stood up. He looked at her. Alice thought his eyes flickered and almost smiled. But he said nothing.

"Robert..."

"Out!" he shouted, pushing her towards the flap.

"No!" shouted Alice, turning back to Robert.

"Tell me what you're doing!" she said.

"Doing my job," said Robert. "I work for Sir Ferdinando Gorges now. We are close to finding the golden city. I will be rich."

"Since when has money mattered so much?" said Alice.

"Since I touched American dollars for the first time. Then I knew. I felt the power."

Alice shook her head. Robert did not look drugged. He seemed to know what he was doing.

"Do you remember Squanto and Ethan Allen and the quest, Robert?"

"Yes."

"And do you remember who you are?"

"Of course. But that life has gone now. This is my new life."

"Have they brainwashed you or something?" said Alice.

"Enough talk!" shouted Robert. "Out!"

Alice glared at him. She felt very afraid now. There must be very dark powers at work this time. And she was alone.

10

Sky Lion and Shadowheart

The snow was hard under foot. Alice slipped several times. At least she still had her own boots underneath but she kept tripping on the long dress. Robert did not help her. He scowled and pushed her harder.

He thrust her through the flap of a huge tent and retreated into the darkness. Through the smoke from the fire, Alice could see that many people were seated in a semi-circle. Two Native Americans sat together. They squatted on fur mats rather than the wooden benches favoured by the Englishmen. They were older than Squanto. Tall feathers crowned their painted, shaven heads. Despite the cold, Alice could see their bare chests painted with red streaks. They wore loin cloths and leather leggings under soft elk-skin blankets decorated with tassels and turquoise beads.

Sir Ferdinando stood up.

"Impressive, my dear," he said slyly, looking at Alice. His hooded eyes burned into her soul. "Come. Sit by the fire."

Alice perched on the wooden bench as best she could, struggling with the hooped layers of her dress. She knew the Indians were watching her.

"You have choices, my dear," said Gorges, sitting down next to Captain Hunt.

"What choices?" said Alice. She tried to sound brave. Her heart was thumping in her ears.

"To stay with me, as my new child bride, and return to England on the next ship. It will be ready in two days once the cargo is loaded. Or go with our red-skinned friends here. These two are my special scouts."

"Your spies?" said Alice, bravely.

Captain Hunt laughed.

"She's too smart to make a good wife, Sir Ferdinando," he said. "Pretty though. Our friends here will trade much cargo for her."

"I suppose your cargo is Indian slaves?" said Alice.

"The cargo is mostly timber and fur. It is much prized in Europe," said Gorges. "Tobacco will be my biggest profit maker, though, once I have thrown the savages off the land I need for my plantations. I shall be rich even if we do not find Norumbega. I shall take a few red-skinned savages, yes. But the Indians are mostly too wild, or too lazy, to make good slaves, unfortunately. No matter. I shall be bringing black slaves from Africa who will do the job very nicely."

"But this is *their* country," said Alice, pointing at the Indians. "You're taking it from them."

"We give them much in return," said Gorges. There was a mocking tone in his voice now.

"Like what, exactly?" said Alice.

"Like Christianity...and guns...oh, and don't forget the liquor," said Gorges. He looked at Captain Hunt and smiled. "It's what these people want. They don't prize gold as we do. Besides, there's no need to be so pious with us, young woman. Before white men arrived and started to civilize this country, the savages were killing each other just for fun. They're still at it, one lot raiding another."

"Good job," smirked Captain Hunt quietly. "Don't want them to club together now, do we?"

"Now what is your decision, Alice?" said Gorges.

"I'm sure you'd like to stay with me. Think of all the fashionable gowns I could give you."

"No thanks!" said Alice. "Not in a million years! I'd rather wear the soft leather tunics of the Native Americans than this garbage any day!"

She tore off her ruff and threw it on the ground.

"Very well," said Gorges. "But do not expect anyone to ransome you."

He turned to the two Native Americans and bowed.

"A gift, my friends," he said, gesturing at Alice.

The two Indians stood up and walked over to Alice. The first took her jaw and bared his teeth, gesturing for her to do the same to see if she had strong teeth.

Alice shrugged away from him.

"My teeth are fine thank you," she said. "Let's just go, shall we. I want to get as far away from these pompous, gold-digging creeps as possible!"

The Indians nodded to one another and shook hands with Sir Ferdinando.

"Outside!" said one of the Indians.

Alice stomped out of the tent. She was very afraid but she didn't want anyone to see that.

There were two horses tied outside the tent. The first Indian lifted Alice onto the front of the blanket saddle and leapt up behind her while the other one spoke briefly to Sir Ferdinando before shaking his hand. Alice's Indian gathered the reins and the horse walked on. As it broke into a trot, and made for the darkness of the trees, Alice could hear the evil, barking laugh of Captain Hunt fading on the wind behind her.

There was no saddle. They were riding bare-back. Alice was quite pleased about that. It was a lot more comfortable than some of the medieval saddles she'd had to negotiate on previous adventures and she found it surprisingly easy to settle into the horse's rhythm. Her Indian wrapped another blanket around her to keep her warm. Alice noticed he had a tomahawk strapped to his waist. He urged the horse on and they broke into a canter, passing trees that threw eerie shadows on the snow in the cold twilight of the mountain night.

She heard the sound of the other horse's hoofs not far behind.

"What is your name?" she asked her Indian.

"Epanow," said the Indian.

"Mine's Alice Hemstock," said Alice.

"I know. But I shall call you *Sky Lion,*" said Epanow.

"Why?" said Alice, secretly feeling excited at her new name.

"Because you speak with the wisdom of a spirit from the skies but would fight like a lion."

"Thank you," said Alice after a pause. "I am honoured. Will Robert get an Indian name?"

"Hmm. *Shadowheart*, perhaps," said Epanow sadly. "For he needs to shed the demons that curtain his true self."

The horse slowed and they stopped.

"We're here," said Epanow.

Alice tried to focus in the gloomy light but her eyes were so cold she thought they might freeze if any tears appeared. Epanow jumped down and gave a low whistle. They waited. Nothing stirred. Epanow whistled again.

Then she heard a hooting sound in the distance. After a minute of silence, the hooting came again, closer now. Something was moving silently towards them.

Then he appeared.

"Squanto!" said Alice. "I'm so pleased to see you!"

Squanto greeted Epanow with a friendly punch and smiled at Alice.

"Gorges and Hunt didn't harm you? No. They wouldn't damage their trophy! Not good for business," said Squanto. He gave a mocking laugh.

"Here. I'll help you down, Sky Lion," said Epanow.

"Oh! I like the name," said Squanto, grinning.

"Do you two know each other?" said Alice.

"Oh, yes!" laughed Squanto. "A deep friendship. We both have had the great misfortune of being captured by Hunt and Gorges. We have had the pleasure of a long voyage on one of His Majesty's ships AND a short holiday on the shores of your homeland. Oh, yes! The apes thought they had us tamed! Gorges thinks we are on his side against our own people. Ha! But enough. Kills Eagle, my other friend here, must take you on to my village and Sachem Massasoit. Epanow and I have another little job. We will have to go back for Robert."

11

Blood Red Jackets

"What's happened to Robert?" said Alice. "He scares me. Really scares me. Has he been drugged?"

"Not really. Robert is acting of his own free will," said Squanto. "But Gorges has the mighty power of the Spirits of Darkness in his hands. He is a powerful Time Regent, and one who has turned to embrace the dark and evil spirits. Robert has shown himself to be interested in the power of wealth. That is his weakness and it has blinded him to Gorges' propaganda. I suppose you would call it brainwashing. Robert has allowed his dark side to triumph over his knowledge of what is good. That could happen to any one of us given the right situation. There is a dark side in all humans. Gorges seeks wealth and through that, power and domination. Few time travellers could resist him. Many have succumbed to his powers."

"I didn't," said Alice.

"No. You are strong and the good spirits have protected you, Alice," said Squanto.

He looked at Alice. She felt a surge of warmth as he smiled at her with his dark eyes.

"You have a deep power," he continued. "You sometimes hear and see things that help you on your quests, don't you?"

"Yes. I suppose I do," said Alice. "But Robert is a good time traveller. I know he is. I think I should come with you to help free him. I think I could get him to turn back."

"No, Alice. Time is running out. Massasoit has

seen visions of William Bradford. In these dreams, William has already started coughing. He has caught plague. You must go to Massasoit. He says you have brought something with you from England from your century. Some powerful medicine that can save William."

"All I have are a few tablets for my arm," said Alice.

"It must be those," said Epanow. "Where are they?"

"I left them in my bum bag," said Alice. "It's back in Bob's chevvy at the liquor store."

Squanto frowned.

"Then you will have to go forward for them," he said.

"So there's no point in me going to Massasoit yet, not without them. Let me come with you to get Robert. You might need me," said Alice.

"Very well. But we must hurry. I'm sure Gorges and Captain Hunt will find out soon that we are taking you to Massasoit," said Squanto.

"I think those two followed us from Boston," said Alice. "The Boston in America, that is. Not the original town of Boston in Lincolnshire, near where I live in England. I did wonder if I was being watched at home though, too."

"So, that's where they went, is it?" said Squanto. "Following you. Massasoit was tracking them in his visions until they masked their movements somehow. Very clever. They intercepted you before we were ready."

"Come on," said Squanto.

He lifted Alice back onto the horse and jumped up behind her. "You really do need to lose this costume," he added, coughing as he pushed the voluminous skirt layers away from his face.

"If you take me back to the tent where I changed, I'd be only too pleased to get my own gear back," said Alice.

Epanow leapt up behind Kills Eagle and they started back towards the English encampment. They did not get far.

Kills Eagle slowed down. They stopped and listened. Then they heard a series of clicks.

Squanto shouted something and Alice suddenly felt herself being roughly dragged from the horse onto the safety of the soft snow. Squanto smacked the horse away into the trees and helped Alice into the cover of undergrowth.

"Muskets!" he whispered. "Stay down!"

Alice fiddled with the fastening and wriggled out of the hooped skirt. She had much more freedom in just the petticoat. Squanto reached for an arrow from his back and rested it in his bow. Alice knew that Epanow and Kills Eagle were nearby.

"Those scheming devils!" hissed Squanto. "They must have tracked you. Good job we didn't lead them to Massasoit."

"Where are they?" whispered Alice.

"I will find them before they find us, do not fear. I can move in silence. Captain Hunt and his soldiers are like bright red buffaloes. They call us red skins because we paint ourselves but that is nothing compared to the scarlet colour of blood that Hunt's soldiers dye their jackets. Stay down!"

In a flash, Squanto vanished. Alice was alone in the freezing forest. She wrapped the discarded skirt around her for more warmth and kept very still, straining to see in the darkness.

Then the shots came. Crackling like fireworks and sparking white in the velvet night. Several. Maybe ten. A few cries. Then nothing. Silence again.

Alice waited. She wanted to stand up. She was so cold now that she worried she might get frozen into an ice sculpture.

She heard a crackle very close and turned. It was Squanto. He was grinning as usual and wiping his knife blade on something hairy. He glanced at Alice.

"Oops. Sorry. Forgot you white people don't like scalps." He threw it down. "Back in my tribe the girls your age collect scalps, Alice."

Alice gulped and stared at Squanto. He grinned.

"Bet you'd get to like it in time. According to Massasoit, we *savages* only scalp our enemies, unlike some men, who scalp the earth. The earth and all its living treasures are our equal, each with its purpose and to be respected. Men who chase golden dreams scalp the beauty of nature itself and offend the spirits. One day, the spirits will desert the earth. There will be nothing left."

Alice watched the young Indian's handsome face. He was usually so full of fun. For a few seconds, pain clouded his eyes.

"Enough!" he snapped. "Let's go. The other two are up ahead."

"But who was after us? Who did you . . . "

"Red coats! I would not liken them to any beast of this earth except themselves. Nothing else is quite so evil or quite so stupid!"

He laughed. He helped Alice back on to the horse and jumped up behind her.

As they trotted along Alice decided not to ask any more questions. Squanto was right. Whoever was chasing them was definitely her enemy. She tried to think of home. But where was home? Did she belong back in England or could she even think of staying here? After a while it would become her home. She would miss her family though, which meant she wouldn't want to stay really. But she liked the way the Indians thought. It was civilized and natural at the same time. In Squanto's world, everything had its right place. Humans did not seem to dominate over other earthly things. That felt good. As a time traveller, Alice wondered what her destiny would hold. Someday, she might have to make a very difficult decision.

They were approaching the settlement now. The three Native Americans jumped from the horses. In silence, Squanto signalled for Alice to stay where she was. She patted her horse's neck and watched her new friends melt into the night once more. She could see the fires and the glow from the tents in the clearing through the low branches of the trees. But it was no good. She couldn't just sit there. She had to help find Robert. Alice slid from the horse onto the snow and edged around the clearing towards the tent where she had changed.

Her petticoat snagged on a bush. Alice pulled on it but that just made a fine curtain of snow tumble from the branches with a patter. She froze. Suddenly she felt a hand across her mouth and another arm around her chest pinning her arms to her sides. She struggled and tried to shout but only made a muffled splutter.

"Sshh! Will you shut up!" said a voice.

She tried to turn.

"Sshh, Alice... aarggh!"

Alice bit the hand that muzzled her. She pulled away from her captor. Her dress ripped as she turned. She was breathing very fast.

"Are you going to kill me then?" she said.

12

Dark Side

Robert glared at Alice, sucking his bleeding finger.

"Of course I'm not going to kill you," he said.

"Well you didn't seem all that bothered about me last time we met," said Alice.

"That was an act."

"I don't believe you. You were doing what Gorges wanted."

"Only to play along with him."

"It was pretty convincing."

"Then I'll try for an *Oscar* someday," said Robert.

They looked at each other in silence.

"Why didn't you give me a signal or something?" said Alice eventually.

"Because you would have behaved differently and given us away. I couldn't risk it. I guessed the Indians were on our side."

Alice scowled at Robert. She didn't know what to believe. Part of her felt guilty that she had mistrusted Robert. But part of her was still suspicious. And she wouldn't have given them away.

"O.K. You are a bit right," said Robert sheepishly. He blushed slightly. "I'm sorry, O.K? I really am. At first I WAS sucked in by Gorges. Maybe it was the influence of evil spirits or something. I did think he had a point about getting rich. The world is lead by rich men. If you can't beat them you may as well join them... well that's what I thought at first. But when I saw you again, I knew I couldn't keep it up. Not really. I... you... well... I just knew! So I started acting, to save both our lives."

Alice stared at Robert. She felt angry and sorry at the same time. For once, she really didn't know what to say.

"You don't trust me, do you?" said Robert. "I can't believe it! After all the adventures we've had together, you really think I could hurt you?"

"I...I'm not sure, Rob," said Alice. "Squanto thought you could."

"I don't care what he thinks! It's what YOU feel that matters to me. I was protecting you. One wrong move and we'd both have been killed."

"So where are Gorges and Captain Hunt now?" said Alice.

"Gone to the coast," said a deeper voice from behind a nearby tree. Squanto stepped out from where he had been watching them. He stared at Robert menacingly. "Apart from the group they sent after us, they've all gone. The place is deserted."

"Why?" said Alice.

"You have time travelled from the liquor store to the early winter in the year 1620. William Bradford and the pilgrims will have landed in the *Mayflower*. And further along the coast, so has the ship Gorges has really been waiting for. The one from Africa," said Squanto.

Alice shivered.

"Slaves," she murmured.

"Yep. That should keep Gorges busy for a while," said Robert.

"How are we going to time travel?" said Alice. "Gorges has the arrowhead Time Trigger."

"But I still have the Spirit Pond rune stone," said Robert. He pulled it from his pocket. "I tricked them earlier."

Alice looked at Robert in surprise. She felt a warm wave of relief swim over her. She smiled at him.

"Shall we return to our own time for the medicine, then?" she asked, turning to Squanto.

"Of course. That is your destiny," said the young Indian.

"Are you coming with us?" said Robert.

"I suppose I could," said Squanto. His eyes narrowed. "Do I need to watch over you, Shadowheart?"

"I am NOT working for them," said Robert. "I wouldn't go over to their side. Not really."

"Everyone has their own dark side, Robert," said Squanto. "We could all be tricked to cross over within ourselves by the Spirits of Darkness. And especially by Gorges. He is more evil than anyone I have ever known." He looked at Robert. The two young men stared at each other. "But no," said Squanto eventually. "I think you have crossed back to us. It is safe for me to stay here for now and go back to Sachem Massasoit. He will be able to see into your time and watch over you. He'll help me make a Time Tunnel and come to you if anything goes wrong."

"Right. Let's go," said Robert.

"Just a sec," said Alice. "I can't go back to the liquor store and Bob and your parents dressed like this. I'll only be a minute..."

She turned towards Gorges' tent.

"Watch out for Robert, Sky Lion," whispered Squanto in Alice's ear as she walked past him.

Alice glanced at Robert. He was looking at them. She smiled weakly. In her heart, she believed in Robert. He had been engulfed by evil but now he was back. But he had shown how easily a time traveller could turn. They must always be on their guard. She gave Squanto a small nod and dived into the tent to change back into her own clothes.

When she re-emerged into the freezing night, the

three Indians and Robert were waiting. There was an awkward silence between them.

"Let's go," said Alice.

She took Robert's cold hand and grinned at Squanto.

"See you soon," she said, closing her eyes.

Once again, Robert and Alice were spinning in a vortex of time travelling brilliance as Robert clutched the Spirit Pond rune stone. Alice concentrated her thoughts on the liquor store on the interstate highway and a moment later, she felt the smooth floor of the vending machine room. She opened her eyes. There was a dollar bill on the ground beside them, in front of the machine with the *Hershey* bars. Robert stooped and picked it up.

"Don't you be throwin' them dollars away, now," joked Bob. "Nickels, dimes and dollars ain't much on their own, but after a while, they sure do mount up into treasure, if you're careful!" He winked at them. "I'll see you in the parking lot. I'm just gonna get your folks from the liquor store."

Alice looked at Robert. He was folding the dollar bill into his wallet. He looked up at her and smiled. That smile. The one that Robert did when he flicked his eyebrows up. That was the Robert she knew and trusted. She breathed a sigh of relief and followed him back out to Bob's truck.

There was no chance at the moment to time travel back with the medicine. She looked behind them into the darkness, but the headlights that had followed them from the airport did not return. So she settled back and listened to Bob. An hour later, they turned off the main road towards the Green Mountains of Vermont.

The snow was thick between the trees along the side of the roads. Alice smiled at a road sign that said 'Moose crossing'.

"Now that there is the *Ben and Jerry's* Ice Cream factory," said Bob, as they passed a building covered in coloured lights.

"*The* Ben and Jerry's?" said Robert.

"Yep. That's where it's made. Right here in Vermont. Best ice cream in the world. And that next building is where you can make your own Vermont Teddy Bear," said Bob. "You can choose a body and have it stuffed and choose his clothes. All kinds of outfits. My wife got me a *Superman* one. They give you a real birth certificate too."

"I hope we get a chance to do that," said Alice.

She looked at Robert. He cringed and shook his head. Alice grinned.

"Do they do *James Bond* ones?" she asked.

Robert smiled sweetly at her and shrugged.

"What about fairy ones?" he said.

Alice stuck her tongue out at him.

"Here we are then, folks," said Bob, pulling up the truck outside a hotel. "This is Stowe. Pretty, ain't it?"

Alice had to agree.

"Cool," she said, jumping down. She slipped slightly.

"Mind yourself, young lady," said Bob.

It was very, very cold. Alice was almost afraid to take a deep breath. She could feel the air chilling her bare face and hands and biting at her legs through her trousers. In the light of the street lamps, Alice could clearly see the church spire at the end of Main Street, framed on either side by the red and yellow clapboard houses with their wooden verandahs and porches. Snowdrifts were piled like marshmallow on top of roofs and in front of picket fences.

A fire blazed in the hotel lobby.

"Guess I'll say goodbye for now," said Bob, shaking Mr Davenport's hand. "You folks give me a call if you need a taxi to take you to a shopping mall or the snowmobile tours or any place else. Oh, and I recommend the pancakes for breakfast. They'll put chocolate or blueberries in them and the syrup from the maple trees around here is as fresh as it gets!"

"Sounds good!" said Robert.

"Would you like a snack?" asked Mrs Davenport at the hotel reception. "There's room service. Apparently they will do us pizzas or burgers before we go to sleep."

Alice and Robert nodded eagerly.

"Here are your room keys," said Robert's dad. "Your rooms are just down the corridor from ours. Leave your bags in one of the rooms and come into our room for the supper. Then we must get some sleep if we're to be up early to collect our skis and boards."

The pizza was huge but Alice was very hungry. Robert's burger and chips vanished very quickly from his plate too.

"Hope I can manage a maple syrup pancake in the morning," said Alice wistfully.

They said goodnight to Mr and Mrs Davenport. Robert had dumped his bag in Alice's room for quickness before the room service had arrived.

"Have you got those tablets?" said Robert as they walked down the corridor.

"Yes," said Alice. "Do you think they are the powerful medicine that can cure William?"

"Don't see what else we could have that could help. Maybe we should time travel now, to take them back to Squanto," said Robert.

"I'm so tired," said Alice, putting her key in the door to her room.

Robert looked up and down the corridor suspiciously.

"Do you think we could have been followed?" said Alice in alarm. She turned the door handle.

"I do," said a deep American voice from inside Alice's room.

Alice's heart jumped. Robert pushed the door wider with one finger.

"Hello!" said Alice.

"How are you?" said Ethan Allen.

He stood up and bowed to Alice, his hat brushing the carpet in front of his boots.

"Fine thank you," said Robert. He looked sternly at the American. "What are you doing here?"

13

Snowmobile

"Gee, now that don't sound too friendly, Robert," said Ethan Allen. "You have gotten ruder since we last met. Guess you must have bumped into Gorges and Hunt earlier and some of their charm rubbed off on you."

He took a step towards Robert and held out his muscular hand. Robert backed away. The American's coat and breeches shed dirty snow on to the carpet.

"Guess I should have worn my sneakers," said Ethan, laughing at the mud as he closed the door. "That's what you call those shoes, ain't it?"

"These are trainers," said Robert.

"I think they are called sneakers in America," said Alice, trying to sound friendly.

"I don't think Robert here is too pleased to see me, Alice," said Ethan. "That doesn't surprise me, mind you. Not after talking to my friend Squanto. He doesn't exactly trust you, Robert. I came here to help you two, but if you'd rather . . ."

"Thanks!" said Alice. "We need all the help we can get."

She scowled at Robert.

"How do we know we can trust *him*?" said Robert.

"You're gonna have to decide, Robert," said Ethan. "And quick. There's trouble on its way. These Green Mountains are my home. I know them better'n any folk. As good as most critters. And you're Brits! You won't stand a chance out there on your own."

"I can ski and snowboard," said Robert.

"Sure you can. But you're gonna need to know where you're going. And in these temperatures a man can die in minutes if he gets exposed."

"Shut up, Robert!" said Alice, ignoring his glare. "What trouble is on its way?"

Just then, there was a shuffling noise outside the door. Ethan Allen lunged towards it and turned the key.

"That trouble! Quick! Get dressed in your thickest things," he said.

For a moment, Robert eyed the door and looked back at Ethan doubtfully. Then he unzipped his bag and put his snow boarding trousers over his combats. Alice struggled into her salopettes and jacket and snatched her hat and gloves.

Someone rattled the door handle.

Ethan sprang over to the window and levered it open. A gust of cold air sailed into the room.

"Quick! Out now!" shouted Ethan.

"Wait!" said Alice. "The medicine!"

She snatched her bum bag and climbed out into the snow after Robert. She put on her hat and fastened the bag around her waist.

The someone was pushing hard against the bedroom door now, trying to break it open.

"This way!" shouted Ethan, running across to a track. Everywhere looked silvery white in the moonlight. Alice struggled in the deep snow as far as the track then ran as fast as she could to keep up with the others. Ethan darted into a red barn that was half buried in a snowdrift.

"Transport!" he said, pulling at a blanket.

"Wicked!" said Robert. "That's more like it."

Underneath the blanket was a big, black snowmobile. Ethan put a tight-fitting hood with an all-in-one facemask under his softer hat, which he tied on top securely. Then he fastened his coat and put on heavy gloves. He leapt astride the saddle and started the engine, revving it to full throttle.

"Get on!" he shouted.

Robert jumped behind Ethan then shuffled back to leave a space for Alice. She squashed in and put her arms around Ethan.

Ethan switched on the headlight and the snowmobile lurched forwards. He span it round at the entrance of the barn and they sped off across a snow covered field towards the base of Mount Mansfield. Where the powder was deep, it was smooth and thrilling but Alice had to grit her teeth over the bumpy bits.

Alice glanced behind. She could hear something that sounded like horses following them. The snowmobile ducked in and out of trees, swerving across a wooden bridge. The horses followed, their hoofs clattering noisily.

Ethan stopped and turned the snowmobile around to face their attackers. He revved the engine. Alice gulped. They were on the top of the steep sides of a high riverbank. The freezing currents swirled between the ice floes beneath them.

The horses slowed. Alice could see Captain Hunt's angry face in front. He suddenly dug his heels into his animal's flank and waved his men on. Ethan revved the snowmobile's engine even louder. One of the horses reared and threw its rider. But Captain Hunt was closing fast.

"Hunt needs to modernise his transportation!" yelled Ethan over his shoulder, laughing.

He turned the snowmobile to face down towards the river then released the throttle. They hurtled towards the icy waters at full speed with snow spraying out on both sides.

"Tell Robert to use the Spirit Pond Time Trigger!" yelled Ethan.

"Rob . . ."

"I heard him. I'm holding it. This should be some journey!" shouted Robert.

Alice felt Robert squeezing her more tightly and she knew they were about to time travel again. It was incredible. Just as the snowmobile was about to hit the water, it lifted off the ground at immense speed. Alice couldn't keep her eyes open. The nausea and spinning were too great. The three travellers were whirling through the centuries in a tunnel that linked them with the past. The power of the Spirits of Time and all the universe surged through them.

"Ow! That hurt," said Alice, wincing as they landed. She opened her eyes. They had flown across the river and skidded to a halt. The engine of the snowmobile stalled. The huge silhouettes of the Green Mountains of Vermont still rose before them. But there were no barns in the fields and no covered bridges. The steeple of the church in Stowe had vanished and there were no flickering town lights.

"What time is this?" said Alice, whispering for no reason.

"Hopefully, we're back in early 1621. Mid winter," said Ethan. "This is frontierland for real. Not many white men have been this far just yet, except the hunters. If we succeed with the quest, more pilgrims will come though. And the rest. There will be a great war for independence from your English king fought here, in my own time, a century from now in 1775. But that's another story. I gotta get you to Squanto before Captain Hunt gets you. Hold tight!"

Ethan started the engine again and they sped off.

The powdered snow was smoother now, undisturbed by the contours of farm tracks and boundaries beneath. They travelled very fast indeed.

Further and further they went, speeding across the white wilderness through the night. Alice dozed against Ethan's back, shielding her face from the cold backdraught. She woke to see a bewildered deer spring for cover. Soon after, she felt the engine slow and the snowmobile stopped.

"From here, we walk," said Ethan.

Alice climbed down. She was stiff and cold.

"Where are we?" said Robert.

"Close to the secret winter camp of the Wampanoag," said Ethan. He started poking about in the undergrowth, "Now where did I put them ... aha!"

He dragged out a bundle of what looked like oversized tennis racquets.

"Snowshoes?" said Alice.

"Correct," said Ethan. "Here. Strap them on tightly over your boots."

It was surprisingly easy to walk in the snowshoes. Alice and Robert followed Ethan in between trees and across a clearing and even over the edge of a small frozen lake. They were able to walk across drifts that would have been up to Alice's waist.

"There are animal tracks here," called Robert.

Ethan stopped to look.

"Umm. Wolf I think. Too big for Coyote. And over there, on that tree trunk, do you see those big scratches?" Alice and Robert nodded. "Bear claws made those."

"Wicked!" said Robert.

Alice looked around nervously.

Robert made growling noises at her.

"Oh don't worry!" said Ethan Allen, laughing at

her expression. "The bears won't wake up for another couple of months. Come on. We're almost there. Aha! There you are my friend!"

"You took your time," said Squanto, emerging on a pathway through the trees. He was grinning. "Glad you left your noisy monster well away from the camp. My people would be terrified of just the vibrations, even if they could not see or hear it. Were you followed?"

"I can't be sure," said Ethan, taking off his snowshoes. "Hunt has developed ways of tracking us, I think. But my machine will be too fast for him to catch up for a while."

"Did you bring the medicine?" said Squanto to Alice.

"Yes," said Alice.

"Then you must follow me," said Squanto.

"I will stay here," said Ethan, stacking up the snowshoes. "To keep watch."

Squanto nodded at his friend and padded off into the trees, silent as ever in his deerskin shoes.

"We must hurry," said Squanto. "My sachem, the mighty Massasoit, would speak with you urgently. William Bradford grows ill. He has caught the plague as the spirits foretold. Time is running out. You must act soon to save him. These plagues have wiped out whole tribes. You must stop it now before it kills us all."

14

Dream Catcher

The camp nestled in a clearing, shielded from the worst of the weather by the tall trees. The white snow camouflaged a circle of domed houses. As they crept invisibly between the dwellings, Alice could see they were made from bent saplings covered with bark and woven mats. They looked sturdy and warm with their sleeping platforms heated by the warmth rising from the fires.

Squanto stooped and entered a slightly larger structure that stood apart from the other dwellings. It smelt of spices and burning logs. Alice and Robert followed. Two figures sat behind the fire. As they stepped closer Alice saw that one was an old man. He was magnificently dressed in white furs with a soft white leather tunic and two enormous white feathers standing high above his head. He wore a necklace of what looked like bear claws on his bare chest. His white beard looked strangely out of place on the face of an Indian. To Alice's surprise, beside him sat Two Bears, the Indian girl who had helped Alice to dress in the English camp. She looked pleased to see Alice.

Squanto sat down cross-legged and bowed towards the older man.

"I am Massasoit," said the grey-haired Native American with wise eyes. "And this is my adopted granddaughter, whom you have already met. Sit. Smoke a pipe with us. There is much to discuss and the night grows shorter."

Alice and Robert sat down on the woven blanket

on the other side of the fire. Alice took off her hat and gloves and unzipped her jacket. Squanto poured cups of sweet smelling drinks for them. It was warm and delicious.

"You have many questions, do you not?" said Massasoit.

"Do you want the medicine?" asked Robert.

"Yes. I have called on the spirits. They have shown me that you have a powerful medicine that will save my people from the white man's disease," said Massasoit.

"The spirits can see into your future?" said Alice.

"Yes. And into yours."

Alice did not reply. She was feeling a little dizzy. Maybe it was the drink or lack of sleep. She could hear the Indian drums again, in the distance.

"Can we have a go at calling the spirits?" said Robert.

Squanto glanced at him in surprise.

"Communing with the spirits is not a game, young Robert," said Massasoit. "And it is not for me to decide. Only for the spirits. You can journey towards them if it is your destiny. You are brave, Robert. But you must temper courage with wisdom. Your enemies will be quick to use you if you do not see clearly."

"Who are my enemies?" said Robert.

Squanto looked at him again and scoffed. The sachem raised a hand in warning.

"Enemies are everywhere," said the great chief. "Large, like the ships that carry guns and soldiers, and small, like the poison that causes plagues. But always there is the enemy within. Your soul battles constantly."

Robert looked a bit sheepish.

Massasoit closed his eyes and took a deep breath.

He rocked gently and raised his hands, humming a chant.

"Knowledge feeds wisdom, my friends," he said. "Seek knowledge of all things and contemplate upon what you find along the path. The spirits will guide your philosophies in the light of reality. There is much beauty in all things but there is no avoiding the darkness and the battles. To war is part of being human, ordinary mortals or time travellers both. It will always happen across all the continents of our world. If attempts to stop war fail, those who survive must strive to change. History can guide us to enrich the future. Chaos can be avoided."

"I don't really understand," said Robert. He yawned.

"You will," said Squanto.

Alice was struggling to focus. She leant back on her hands. The green and gold of the carpet seemed to fuse with the turquoise beading on Massasoit's robe and the swirl of the flames from the fire. Shapes of animals formed in the smoke and danced grotesquely until they vanished under the domed ceiling.

"I...I..."

Alice saw the muffled shape of Two Bears coming towards her and heard the concern in Squanto's voice. Then nothing. Except the drums and the songs. Beautiful, ancient, Wampanoag songs. The rhythm quickened into a frenzy and the flames exploded into a rainbow of visions.

When Alice opened her eyes, she was lying on furs. Daylight flooded through the doorway. She propped herself up. She had a terrible headache.

"Well?" said a soft voice.

She turned to see Squanto crouching by the fire.

"Well what?" she whispered.

"Was it a powerful dream?"

"I don't know." She lay back down. "I can't remember much at the moment. Except the trees. Talking trees with whispering leaves."

Squanto watched her intently.

"You are lucky," he said.

Alice sat up.

"Am I?"

"Yes. You find it easy to reach the spirit world, even if you do not understand yet. It is harder for me. But Massasoit is patient."

"Do you want to be a sachem?" said Alice.

"No. To be chief is not my destiny. I think Two Bears will be the Squaw Sachem one day. But perhaps my path will lead me to the knowledge of a *powachee*. That's a medicine man and prophet. I would like that."

"What about Robert?"

"He, too, went on a journey last night. Massasoit had to help him. He cried out many times in his sleep. He fights his own demons. I think he woke up to find his head a little clearer, thanks to the potion and Massasoit's teaching."

"What's that?" said Alice, pointing to a round leather hoop about the size of a saucer that hung in the doorway. The centre was elaborately woven into a giant leather spider's web and embroidered with shells and turquoise jewels. Feathers and fur dangled from the frame.

"It is a dream catcher," said Squanto. "I made it for you. It will trap bad dreams so they do not reach you but it will let the good dreams through."

Squanto unhooked the dream catcher and gave it to Alice. He sat down in front of her.

"Oh! It's exquisite. Thank you. May I keep it?" she said.

"I would be offended if you did not," said Squanto.

They looked at each other for a moment. Alice felt warm and happy inside.

"Do you like Robert, Alice?" said Squanto.

"Of course."

Squanto looked disappointed.

"Well . . . I think I do," said Alice. "Although he is behaving very strangely."

"Do you think you could like it here, better than in your time?"

Alice looked at Squanto. The round darkness of his eyes melted into the smile lines on the otherwise smooth contours of his tanned face.

"I don't know," she said. "I think the ways of your people are good."

"Many white people who have been captured by native tribes have stayed among us," said Squanto. "Even when their own people have sent ransom money and they could be free."

"I think I can understand that," said Alice.

Squanto smiled at her. He passed her a bowl of grain and milk.

"What's in here?" said Alice. "It won't drug me will it?"

Squanto shook his head and bounced to his feet.

"I expect it is not quite what you are used to eating in the mornings, but it will keep you strong," he said.

Alice prodded the mixture with her finger. She had to agree. It was very different from toast and marmalade. She scooped a little in her fingers and licked it.

"Actually . . . it's good," she said. "It's very sweet."

"Syrup from the maple trees," said Squanto.

Alice was just about to ask for a second helping when someone's silhouette cast a shadow in the light from the doorway.

15

The Totem Stick

"How are you?" said Two Bears cheerfully.

"Fine, thank you," said Alice.

"Massasoit would speak with you when you are ready," said Two Bears. "Shall I take you to the lake to wash? The lake is covered with ice in winter but there is running water at the base of the frozen waterfall."

"Yes please. It sounds good," said Alice, standing up. "Where is Robert?"

"Talking with Ethan. I think those two could be good friends, if Robert is able to resist Gorges' powers. Ethan is probably teaching him tricks for hunting," said Two Bears. "We will meet them presently. Come on. See you later Squanto."

Despite the deep snow, it was warm in the sunlight. Alice followed Two Bears through the village. She did not have a Time Trigger, so everyone could see her. A young brave was lacing sheets of bark through the frame of a canoe. He looked up at her and smiled. Women stirred cooking pots over fires built in stone circles or sat cross-legged pushing sewing needles through fur and moccasin leathers. Children played with dolls or pretend spears and axes. One or two of the youngest children stopped to stare at Alice, but most people greeted her with a smile.

"This is our winter camp," said Two Bears. "In summer we will return to the coast to farm and fish."

Two men emerged from the doorway of a small domed lodge in a cloud of steam and started rubbing snow on their bare skin despite the cold.

"What are they doing?" asked Alice.

"The sweat lodge is for cleansing dirty skin. We pour water over hot coals," said Two Bears, amused at Alice's expression.

"It's a sauna!" said Alice.

They reached the edge of the silver expanse of the frozen lake. Snow covered the deep ice and Wampanoag children and their wolf-like dogs played safely far out on the surface. At one side, a frozen waterfall hugged the icy hillside, its ripples paralysed where they had flowed at the beginning of winter.

"Wow! That's beautiful!" said Alice.

"Look, here at the bottom. Water flows beneath the ice where we have cut holes," said Two Bears.

Alice washed her face in the freezing water. It felt wonderful.

"Why are you called Two Bears?" asked Alice.

"Massasoit found me in a bear cave when I was very small," said Two Bears. "Two bears were living there too. My parents were murdered. No-one knows whether it was another tribe or white men but I know I am Abenaki from the clothes I wore. Massasoit says that the bear is my totem. It protects me."

Alice smiled in admiration.

"I wonder if I have a totem," she said.

"Of course you do," said Two Bears. "We all do. Perhaps you should ask Massasoit."

Alice nodded. Having her own totem sounded very exciting.

Two Bears led her back through a forest path. Smoke rose in front of them. Through the trees Alice could see Massasoit's birch bark house. The snow had been cleared around it and a fire burned. Squanto was turning a spit. A wonderful cooking smell greeted Alice as they walked closer.

"We will be having a feast tonight in your honour," said Two Bears. "Squanto roasts a deer. There will be much dancing."

Robert was sitting with Ethan Allen. Alice noticed Kills Eagle was there too, carving arrow shafts with his knife. She also saw the fleeting blush on Two Bears' cheeks when Kills Eagle smiled at her.

"Aha," said Robert. "The dreamer awakes."

"I hear you had a few dreams yourself last night," said Alice.

Robert looked down, avoiding Alice's eyes.

"Umm. I think I'll avoid Massasoit's drinks in future," he said. "Hey! I'm looking forward to this party tonight." He was obviously changing the subject.

"Are you O.K.?" asked Alice softly.

Robert looked at her.

He was about to say something when the door of the house opened. Massasoit stepped out, squinting in the sunshine. He held a small, rectangular box in front of his eyes. The side against his face was cut away so he could see through two slits cut in the thin wood on the opposite side. Alice frowned.

"What's he doing?" she said.

"I think you would call those sunglasses," said Squanto. "With these boxes we can still see through the slits but the glare of the sun's rays is excluded."

"That's really clever," said Alice.

"Cool shades," said Robert, grinning. "Not sure I'd want to wear them on the ski slopes though!"

Massasoit had changed his fur robe. This one was made from the colourful pelts of foxes and beavers.

"Sit," said Massasoit.

When everyone was seated around the fire,

Massasoit spoke.

"Alice and Robert have been given this quest and we must help them," he said gravely. "They have travelled the highways of time to bring powerful medicine to stop the plague and save William Bradford. We in turn will do our part to build a bridge between our peoples that will generate the spirit of a new nation."

Alice reached inside her bum bag for the antibiotic tablets.

"I have the tablets," she said.

Massasoit was smiling mischievously. He started chuckling.

"They are not the answer to the conundrum," he said.

"But the quest . . ." said Robert. "We have to save William Bradford with these tablets."

"This drug is what you call a penicillin. It does not kill plague. These are not the powerful medicine that you possess," said Massasoit.

"Well, what is? We didn't bring any thing else," said Robert.

"Yes you did," said Massasoit. "One of you did. You have brought something from your time to ours that will save William. Your dreams will help you. You must go forward to your time and bring the real medicine to me."

Alice looked at Robert. He shrugged at her.

"For the moment, you two must learn a great skill. I think you are ready," said Massasoit. "I will show you something that will give you great power. You must learn how to travel through the dimension of time using a Time Tunnel."

"YES!" said Robert.

"Do we need a Time Trigger as well?" said Alice.

"With practice, some Regents are able to harness

their special powers without a Trigger, but it is easier with one to begin with," said the chief. "And safer. And you two will definitely not be able to travel from the space-frame in the cosmos that you occupy to somewhere else on this planet unless you use a Trigger. Some travellers never succeed with that feat."

"You mean we can travel geographically speaking as well as in time?" said Alice. "We've never done that before."

"Yes. You can command a *roving* Time Tunnel," said Massasoit. "If you are confident and focused and the power of the Spirits of Time is with you, all the dimensions of space-time are at the disposal of a Time Traveller. Although, as you know, it is not advisable to travel forwards in time unless it is as the direct requirement of a quest."

"Well, I already have my Spirit Pond rune stone," said Robert, holding up the Time Trigger.

"Indeed," said Massasoit. "So we must give Alice a Time Trigger." He nodded at Squanto who opened a pouch and took something out. He stood up and gave it to Alice.

It was a small totem pole, delicately carved into the shape of many tiny animals, with a bird on the top. Three deer hoofs were fastened to the base with a leather strap. They rattled as it moved.

Alice was thrilled.

"Is this an Indian instrument?" she said.

"I would not say *Indian*," said Massasoit kindly. "It was carved by an ancient shaman of mixed tribal and Norse descent. One of my ancestors. It was not until hundreds of years later that more Europeans landed on these shores in search of treasure and took it for the Indies. They called us Indians by mistake then, but the name has stayed, and will do across the globe for many generations."

"Would it be more correct to call you Native Americans?" said Robert.

Squanto tried to conceal a splutter of amusement. Massasoit shook his head and smiled.

"To be correct you should call us by our tribe's name, for our people were here long before this land was called America. My people are the Wampanoag federation of tribes. That is our name. Two Bears' people, the Abenaki, came from a bit further north and are themselves divided into smaller tribes," said Massasoit. "My ally, the great Sachem Pasaconnoway, is chief of the Pennacooks tribe. We are many peoples but we were the first human inhabitants of the land that Sir Ferdinando Gorges thinks he owns. Passaconoway has seen the pathway that leads into the future when he talks with the spirits. He has warned how our tribes should join together or we will be destroyed and rooted off the earth. Our peoples do not understand what your cultures call *ownership*. Everything belongs to all creatures, from the land and the sea to the objects we use to hunt or the jewellery we wear. We do not understand this word *mine*. And we do not fence the land as your people do.

"We have lived on this continent that you now call *America* for many generations since our ancestors walked across the glacial plains in ancient times. The name America is very recent and is the white man's choice. It comes from the name of one of the first European settlers to this continent."

"I was wondering about that," said Alice.

"Now. You must continue with your quest. Hold your Time Triggers," said Massasoit. "I want you to close your eyes and turn your inner eyes towards the very centre of your being. Can you do that?"

Robert closed his fingers over the rune stone and Alice squeezed the totem stick in both hands. With her eyes shut, she tried to do what Massasoit had asked.

"I don't get it," said Robert, breathing out.

"Don't hold your breath," said Massasoit. "Breathe naturally. Listen to the sounds of the forest and listen to the air as it passes inside you from the cosmos. When you are relaxed, try breathing first through one nostril, then the other."

Alice reached up and blocked one nostril with her hand, switching sides after each breath. After about ten breaths, she began to relax.

"When you feel strong, switch your thoughts to your own time, open your eyes and draw a circle from the ground on one side and over your head to the other side. When you have travelled, do the same and you will come back to us again. With practice, you will be able to do it quickly."

Alice breathed. In and out. Close the nostril. In and out the other side. Close the nostril. In and out again. She started to feel her special power rising inside her body and she opened her eyes. Just as she was about to touch the totem stick on the ground she heard a shout.

Kills Eagle, who had been standing guard, yelled something that Alice and Robert could not understand. But Squanto could. So could Ethan Allen and Two Bears. In a flash they were standing together in a protective wall. Squanto and Two Bears held up their tomahawks. Ethan drew muskets from his jacket and Kills Eagle pulled an arrow from the quiver on his back.

16

Eggs Sunny Side Up

Massasoit rose slowly to his feet. Alice saw that he held another carved stick in one hand. The shaft was white and the razor sharp tip was the beak of a raven. Feathers, fur, hair, horns and claws dangled along the length. As he lifted it above his head, the great chief shook the wand. It made a sound like a rattlesnake. He whooped and chanted.

Something was approaching through the trees. The undergrowth shook as it was trampled by many horses. A warning shot rang out, echoing back and forth in the forest.

The first rider emerged. It was Captain Hunt. He reined his horse to a stop. More than a dozen soldiers on horseback joined him in a line of gold and red.

The first sound was laughter. Cruel, sneering laughter.

"Savage fools!" cackled Captain Hunt. "You chose your friends badly, Robert. Do you now wish to change your mind and work for Sir Ferdinando with me? As Gorges says, you would make a good disciple. Our powers could combine to make a mighty team. The riches of so many centuries are there for us to plunder. What do you say?"

Alice looked at Robert. His face was black.

"Do you think I am like you?" said Robert bravely. "Well you're wrong! I may have briefly danced on the dark side, but last night I went on a journey into the spirit world and rediscovered my destiny. It is not to work for you. I now know you for the evil cowards that you are!"

Captain Hunt frowned.

"What strength can these savages offer?" he said. "Even the clueless pilgrims could outwit them!"

"You are the savages!" said Robert, almost spitting with anger. "You and Gorges! You come to steal these peoples' land in the name of the king on your own savage pilgrimage for gold. How dare you! These peoples' strength lies in their kindness and in their cunning. You may have guns but you will not defeat them!"

Alice stared at Robert. Captain Hunt was silent too, momentarily stunned by Robert's passion.

"Welcome back, Robert," muttered Ethan under his breath.

Squanto's eyes flicked towards Robert too, before returning his full attention to the attackers.

"As you wish, Robert," sneered Captain Hunt. "Prepare to die! Your chanting chief cannot make medicine that will stop our guns."

Captain Hunt lifted his arm, signalling to his men and Alice heard the clicking of the muskets as they prepared to fire.

Massasoit's chant became an angry shout. He opened his eyes and shook his rattling wand just once, then lowered it with the point on the ground. He dragged it in an oval on the snowy forest floor. The noise from the men and horses suddenly vanished as if someone had switched off the volume on a television set.

"What's happened to them?" said Alice.

They were frozen behind a dusty tunnel wall that encircled them in a shape that resembled the one Massasoit had drawn in miniature on the ground.

"Ha, ha! Strong magic!" said Squanto. "Our chief cannot make powerful medicine, eh?"

He bowed to Massasoit.

Massasoit looked pleased with himself.

"Where shall I send them?" he said quietly.

"Into my time," said Ethan Allen. "My Green Mountain Boys will take care of them."

Massasoit nodded and closed his eyes. He chanted again, tracing over the drawing with the raven beak on his stick.

Alice felt the ground shudder and a tidal wave of power coursing through her. There was a loud crack and the Time Tunnel vanished, taking Captain Hunt and his soldiers with it.

"That was a pretty neat trick, Sir," said Robert. "Can we learn that too?"

"No, young Robert," said the great sachem. "You are much too inexperienced in your art. One day, perhaps, but it is a gift seldom bestowed on time travellers in this universe."

Robert pursed his lip and shrugged.

"What's going to happen to them?" said Alice.

"My men will deal with them," said Ethan Allen.

"I would not count on them disposing of Captain Hunt that easily, Alice," said Squanto. "The rest maybe. But Hunt is as slippery as an eel. He will be back soon. He and Gorges want to kill you and Robert, and take your medicine."

"Yes, my friend may be right," said Ethan. "I think it would be wise to act speedily."

"Sadly, there is no time for you two to stay and dance with us around our fire and feast. Not yet," said Massasoit. "You must return to your own century. It is time for you to command a roving Time Tunnel and use it to take you to your own time and the town of Stowe. Use one of your Time Triggers."

"Right," said Alice, holding up the totem stick.

"Time to learn a new trick!"

Robert grinned at her.

"We will see you all again, won't we?" said Alice suddenly. She noticed Squanto smiling at her. Alice glanced at Robert and saw that he too had seen the fondness in Squanto's eyes. Robert checked himself and concentrated on what Massasoit was saying.

"Oh, yes," said Sachem Massasoit. "I will be watching you. Now go. Control you breathing."

Alice took Robert's hand. She smiled at him then closed her eyes. She started to breathe as Massasoit had taught them, in and out in a slow rhythm. She felt her heart rate slow and her breaths deepen. She stopped listening to the sounds around her and sank deeper within herself. She crouched down and touched the totem stick on the floor before raising it over their heads. Alice started to see the hotel in Stowe where they wanted to be. She touched the stick on the ground on the other side and felt the wind in her face as she was lifted up and spun around without actually moving.

It was a time travelling journey like no other they had made. The colours sparkled in the white heat of the power. Every atom of Alice's being felt as if it was being squashed into the smallest place and then sucked out again, pulling with it her life forces. It was like being driven at one hundred miles an hour over a hump backed bridge. The sinking feeling in her stomach was terrible and fantastic all at once.

Then it stopped. She slowly opened her eyes and blinked in the sunlight streaming through the dining room window.

"Ah! There you are," said Mrs Davenport. "You're dressed for the ski slopes. Good. I didn't think you'd miss breakfast."

Alice looked at Robert and they tried not to giggle. But his mother had seen them.

"What is so funny, Robert?" she snapped, brushing invisible crumbs from her pink salopettes. "Come and sit down at once. Put that dirty stick thing under the table, Alice. Waiter! My son is ready now."

"What'll you have?" said the waiter.

"Everything!" said Robert, studying the menu. "Eggs, bacon, hash browns, pancakes..."

"How would you like your eggs? Easy over or sunny side up?" said the waiter.

Robert looked at Alice for help, but she shrugged. She didn't know what 'easy over' meant either.

"I'll try sunny side up, I think," said Robert.

"And for you, Ma'am?" The waiter looked at Alice.

"Oh, I'll have the same," she said. "And maple syrup and blueberries on the pancakes."

"My. You are hungry!" said the waiter. "Been up all night having adventures or something?" he added.

Alice looked at him closely. But he didn't look familiar. She decided he was just joking. She didn't dare to look at Robert, though, in case they laughed and Robert's mum told them off again.

17

Talking Trees

When the breakfast came a few minutes later it was delicious.

"So. Are you going to catch the shuttle bus up to the mountain and check out the snow?" said Robert's dad in his usual friendly manner. Alice nodded in between mouthfuls. "You can stop off at the hire shop and pick up your skis and Robert's snowboard. We booked them on the way down to breakfast. And don't forget your sun cream. It might be seven degrees below zero outside, but the sun is out."

"I'm going to look in those shops opposite the hotel before we go skiing," said Robert's mum. She pushed back her chair and strode out of the hotel dining room.

"See you over the road in the shops in fifteen minutes?" said Mr Davenport, rushing to catch up with his wife.

Alice swallowed the last gorgeous mouthful of blueberry pancake drizzled in maple syrup and sat back, smiling contentedly.

"What is the medicine that we have?" said Robert.

Alice closed her eyes.

"Massasoit said we have to use our dreams," she said. "I dreamed about trees. Beautiful tall trees. Talking trees. They spoke to me. What did you dream about last night?"

"You don't want to know," said Robert.

"Yes I do," said Alice, flicking her eyes open. "It could be important."

Robert looked at her for a moment.
"It had to do with chopping out dead wood. Making whole again. It made me realise how foolish I had been to listen to Sir Ferdinando Gorges."
"Hmm. Chopping. What did you chop with?"
"I don't know. An axe, I suppose. Or a saw. Lumberjacks use great big tree cutting machines. I've seen them at a paper mill."
"That's it!" said Alice. "Talking trees! That's what our dreams meant."
Robert looked at her blankly.
"What do we use trees for?" said Alice.
"Wood?"
"Ye-es. What else?"
"Paper?"
"Exactly! Talking trees that have been chopped down. Paper makes books and when you read them, they tell you things. Books are talking trees! And we do have a book!" said Alice. She stood up.
"What book?" said Robert.
"The one Dr Sedall gave me. He was telling me to look things up in books. We can find out what the cure for plague is in the little medical book and take that back to William Bradford. The modern book, my talking tree, is the powerful medicine really."
"Sounds reasonable. But where are we going to get whatever cures plague in Stowe?" said Robert.
"I don't know yet. We'll think of something. Come on!"
They walked back down the hotel corridor. Mr and Mrs Davenport were walking towards them on their way out to the shops.
"There's some ski races later on today," said Robert's dad. "The hotel manager says that if you want to enter you have to collect your racing bibs and numbers at the ski school by the chairlift at

lunchtime. I said you two would be keen, as you're good skiers. Here's a voucher for equipment if you two want to go ahead." Mr Davenport sneaked a sideways look at his wife. "We might be a while at the shops."

"Thanks Dad," said Robert, grinning.

Alice was already unlocking her room.

"Here it is," she said, pulling the little medical book from her suitcase. She flicked through the first few pages until she came to the contents page. "Which chapter do you think plague will be under?"

"How about *infectious* diseases?" said Robert, studying the index.

Alice turned to the chapter and skimmed through the disease headings.

"Yep. Here it is. Bubonic plague."

Robert looked over her shoulder. They both read through the description.

"Yuk! Nasty!" said Robert.

"It's like that nursery rhyme. *Ring-a-ring-o-roses*," said Alice. "It says here the victims get a red rash, then they sneeze and cough with pneumonia, then they die."

"Wonder which bit William's got up to?" said Robert. "The sneezing bit, do you think?"

Alice frowned at him.

"That's not funny," she said. "Look. The treatment is either an injection or tablets of something called *tet-ra-cy-clines* which are quite different from penicillins, obviously. Wonder how we can get hold of some tetracyclines?"

"Let's go shopping," said Robert. "I think we should ask at the chemist. They call them drug stores in America, don't they?"

"Good idea," said Alice.

She stuffed the book in the pocket of her ski jacket as they walked out of the hotel. They waited for a yellow school bus to pass before crossing the street to the parade of shops. Alice looked suspiciously at everyone they met. But everybody was friendly.

"They like telling you to 'have a nice day' in America, don't they," said Robert. "I'm tempted to say 'no, I won't', next time someone says it!"

"Let's have a look in here," said Alice, peering in the dark window of a shop called 'Virginia's cavern.'

"What does it sell?" said Robert.

"Books. And patchwork. And those look like interesting stones and pottery and stuff," said Alice.

She pushed the door open. A little bell tinkled at the counter. There was no one about. The chaotic interior of the dimly lit shop had a familiar spicy smell that Alice couldn't quite recognise. Beyond the shelves of patchwork quilts and cushion covers and books and magazines was a ramshackle assortment of exotic wares.

"It really is like a cave in here," whispered Alice.

"Wonder who Virginia is?" said Robert, fiddling with a wooden toy.

Alice started to examine a basket of interesting gems when the curtain in the doorway behind the counter was pushed back. Alice gasped.

"Hello again," said the young woman. "We wondered how long it would take you to find us."

18

Sleighs, Skis and Chairlifts

Two Bears grinned at Alice and Robert. She was casually dressed in jeans and a T-shirt. Instead of plaits, her long black hair fell in waves over her shoulders.

"You look different," said Robert.

"I guess so. Better or worse?" said Two Bears.

"Umm... different... nice different," said Robert, blushing slightly.

"Are you Virginia?" said Alice.

"Yep. And I think you know my grandfather, Rusty?"

The curtain parted again and Massasoit appeared, his white hair tied back in a ponytail over a denim jacket.

"Rusty?" said Alice. "Where did that name come from?"

"I figured I had red hair when I was a young man on the reservation," said the chief, grinning mischievously. "Always fancied red hair!"

"How long have you had this shop?" said Alice.

"Not long. We took it over when it became empty and blended into the local community to wait for you to arrive at the hotel. Good camouflage?" said the elderly Time Regent.

"Brilliant!" said Robert.

"Actually, I rather like it here in the shop. So much to play with," said Massasoit. "I like some of your ...umm...gadgets. Like this machine that plays music from little round discs."

"It'll be a pity when we go back to our own time

for good," said Two Bears. "I've made some friends at the junior high school in town. And they do great candy in your time! Not to mention fries. Oh, and peanut butter and jelly sandwiches!"

"Urgh! They don't sound good!" said Robert, screwing up his nose. "You wouldn't get them in England!"

"I would like to see your England," said Two Bears. "I have seen pictures of London. I hope I have a quest that will take me across the ocean one day."

"England has a lot more good stuff than Big Ben and Buckingham Palace, you know," said Alice.

"Yeah. Ancient castles and *Cadbury's* chocolate!" said Robert.

"You must show me," said Two Bears.

"Anytime!" said Robert.

"I'll put the closed sign on the door and we can go downstairs to talk," said Two Bears, smiling.

"Come," said Massasoit, leading them down the narrow stairway behind the curtain.

The cellar was converted into a cosy apartment. Alice noticed the same type of woven rugs on the floor that she had seen in Massasoit's birch bark house in the seventeenth century. Embroidered medicine bags hung along the wall with head-dresses, pipes and a selection of knives. Two pairs of moccasins were arranged neatly beside the fire. Animal skins stretched across the wall, decorated with elaborate drawings and markings hand-painted on them. There was a pleasant smell of incense and home cooking.

"Wow! I bet you sell a lot of genuine old Indian relics," said Robert, looking around approvingly.

"Yes. We have a good supplier," said Two Bears.

Massasoit chuckled and winked at them.

They sat down on some comfy, modern armchairs.

"Let us talk," said the great chief. "I think you have something to tell me."

He listened as Alice described their dreams and how they had lead them to look in the book for the answer. He nodded and smiled. Alice passed him the medical book.

"You make a good team," he said. "You could be wise and powerful Time Regents one day. So. Talking trees! The great medicine that you bring is knowledge, the knowledge that you find in books." He chuckled to himself. "Making symbols that speak to others is a way of talking across the centuries. My ancestors have drawn on the walls of caves and on skins. This paper that comes from trees is very clever. But the trees might suffer if man takes too many."

Alice sighed and nodded.

"Now, my young friends," said Massasoit, tapping the textbook. "We must find some of this *tetracycline*."

Then he stopped and listened. Someone was moving around in the shop above them.

"Did you lock the door?" he asked Two Bears.

"Oh, yes," she whispered.

"Then we have uninvited guests," said Massasoit.

He strode across to the wall and pulled down some weapons. He threw a knife and axe to Two Bears and picked up the white, carved staff with the raven totem.

The noises above grew louder. There was a thud and the sound of breaking china.

"That was unnecessary," muttered Two Bears crossly.

She unlocked a back door and Robert and Alice followed her out into the courtyard.

"Aren't you coming?" said Alice, turning back to Massasoit.

"No. Don't worry about me. This is my destiny. Two Bears will take you far away. Go!"

Robert and Two Bears opened the doors to a stable next to a red barn.

"Horses!" said Alice in surprise. "*Shire* horses?"

"Say hello to Burt and Paul," said Two Bears, fixing the harness to the sleigh. "They're Belgian horses, not Shires. But they're very similar. We do sleigh rides for tourists at weekends. And dog sledding."

"Are you proposing that we escape from Captain Hunt in a sleigh?" said Robert, gaping.

"It's one of the best ways to get around town in deep snow, trust me," said Two Bears. "Hop aboard!"

Robert frowned but he followed Alice and Two Bears up onto the seat at the front.

"Put your hats on and goggles," said Two Bears. "There's going to be a lot of spray once we clear the side walk."

She picked up the reins and drove the two horses on. The sleigh lurched forwards and began to gather speed. Alice gripped the rail at the edge of the seat as the horses picked their way around a restaurant parking lot and out to the fields behind. The sleigh glided smoothly over the snow, occasionally bouncing them off their seat as it clipped a ridge. They were speeding towards Mount Mansfield, parallel to the main road. They passed snow covered clapboard houses with yellow and blue shutters and quaint red barns, half buried in snowdrifts. There was even a real covered wooden bridge. It looked just like the photographs in the travel brochures.

"I need to get us close to the mountain. Ethan will

meet us there," shouted Two Bears above the bells of the sleigh and the horses' hoofs.

Robert looked behind them.

"No sign of trouble yet," he said.

It was starting to snow.

"Hope your grandfather is O.K.," said Alice.

"Oh, don't worry about him," said Two Bears. "He'll be having a great time!"

Suddenly, they heard a gun shot coming from the trees in front of them.

"Oops! That's trouble!" said Two Bears, pulling on the reins and swerving the sleigh to the right.

The sleigh tilted dangerously. Alice gripped her seat. The horses cantered now, bouncing the sleigh over the edges of paths and driveways.

"Cor! That hurt!" said Robert, as they slammed back down onto the seat.

"Do you see that building over there?" shouted Two Bears, pointing. "It's the chairlift. Ethan and Squanto should be at the bottom. I'll get you as close as I can!"

"Why don't we just use the Time Triggers and escape?" shouted Robert through the snow.

"You don't know where to go," said Two Bears. "We must wait for the others to take you. Massasoit did not have time to tell you everything."

A second shot rang out and a bullet whistled close to their heads.

"I think I see them," said Alice. "Yes! Over there. It's Ethan. He's got some skis."

Two Bears turned the horses once more and they flew towards the side of the chairlift. She slowed the horses as they approached the car park. A few skiers turned to look. Alice and Robert jumped down.

"I'll keep our attackers busy as a decoy for as long as I can," yelled Two Bears, geeing on the horses again before Alice or Robert could protest.

"Over here!" shouted Ethan Allen. "Get your skis on Alice."

He passed her some ski boots and skis.

"What about me? I'm better riding a board . . . aha! Cool!" said Robert, grinning as Squanto passed him a shiny snowboard decorated with a white wolf. He strapped one boot on.

"Quick! Onto the chairlift," said Squanto. "Hunt won't follow us up there. He can't ski!"

They side-stepped up the slope to the lift. Luckily there was no queue.

"Let us go in front and you two pretend to mess up getting on the chair. That will leave an empty one for us. The attendants can't see us, remember," said Ethan.

Robert grinned. He pretended to tread on one of Alice's skis and they let the first double chair go past them for Ethan and Squanto. Alice and Robert turned to face the mountain and waited for the next chair. Alice felt it on the backs of her knees and she sat back next to Robert. He pulled over the safety bar and they rested their skis and board on the bottom rail as the chair lift pulled them high above the snow towards the top of the mountain.

19

Flickering

Alice looked back.

"There he is!" she said. "And he doesn't look very happy."

Captain Hunt was standing on the edge of the platform waving his fist angrily at them.

"Ooh! You might be invisible to everybody else, but I wouldn't stand there . . . " said Robert, wincing.

"Oh, dear," said Alice, just as the next chairlift smacked into Captain Hunt and sent him flying over the edge of the platform into the deep snow below.

"Now he's going to be really mad!" said Robert, laughing. "Get ready to jump off and ski for your life at the top, Alice."

Alice checked the fastening on her skis and pulled her goggles over her hat. She skied off the lift and over to where Squanto and Ethan were waiting. Ethan was flicking the last catch on his ski boots.

"Cool gear," said Robert, admiring Squanto's snowboard. "You're a man of many talents."

"So are you, my friend," said Squanto. Alice was pleased that the two young men were friends at last.

"Keep your Time Triggers handy," said Ethan. "If you get into trouble from our enemies, breathe in and out, think of the power you wield, and you will be able to travel in and out of time to escape your attackers."

"You mean sort of switch-about-time-travel?" said Robert excitedly.

"I suppose so. I call it flickering," said Squanto. "It's a lot of fun, but very hard work. Hope you're fit."

Robert scowled at him in a friendly way.

"Let's go then," said Ethan. "I will take you to my secret hideaway in the mountains."

Robert rode his board after Ethan, following in the tracks of his skis, and Alice pushed herself off. Apart from a few visits to the dry slope at home, she hadn't skied for a while and she was relieved to find that she was still a pretty good skier. Squanto followed at the rear.

Alice kept a good distance between her skis and Robert. His speedy turns were sending flumes of fresh powder on either side. They were travelling very fast and the snow was fantastic. There were no icy patches and Alice relaxed as she concentrated on keeping her skis parallel as she turned across some of the steeper slopes of the marshmallow white alpine meadows.

Then she heard it. It was a low rumbling sound at first. She knew exactly what it was. Snowmobiles. Several of them. The whine of their engines was closing fast. She glanced behind. Captain Hunt might not be able to ski but he had no problems manoeuvring a snowmobile on a mountainside. Neither did his two associates.

She saw Squanto waving something, then he vanished.

"He's *flickering*!" she muttered.

She put her two ski poles in one hand and reached into her jacket pocket with the other, keeping her eyes on the trail ahead.

"Rob! Use your Trigger! Go back to 1621!" she yelled, as she squeezed the little totem stick.

She would normally close her eyes when she travelled, but she kept them open as she was moving so fast. She didn't want to hit a tree in this century or any other. She took a breath and switched her thoughts inwards.

Nothing happened. She could hear the snowmobiles behind closing on her. She tried again. This time, she felt a wave of heat pass through her. There was a rapid flash and she felt as if she had skied over a bump. But the noise behind had gone. So had Robert in front. She glanced behind and saw Squanto grinning at her under his sunglasses. Then Ethan appeared, snaking in rapid turns on the slope below her. Where was Robert? Perhaps he hadn't heard her shouting.

She was just beginning to worry when he appeared. He was right in front of her.

"Watch it!" she yelled. "You've slowed down."

She had to use all the power in her legs to drive her skis round and avoid crashing into Robert. But she made it. He grinned at her and gave her the thumbs up sign. For a couple of turns, they skied and boarded side by side, before Robert broke off and rode his board down towards Ethan.

Then she heard it again.

"He's followed us!" shouted Alice.

Captain Hunt was close behind Squanto now. Alice could see his evil grin and bushy eyebrows below his helmet.

She turned back and gripped her Time Trigger again. In another flash, she flick time travelled again as she skied. She was ready this time, and she bent her knees well into the slope of the mountain to take the impact as she skied over the invisible bump that bridged space and time. She could see the wires of the chairlift. She was back in the twenty-first century but the slopes were deserted in the blizzard.

Once again, the others did the same. And so did Captain Hunt.

Alice felt a bolt of evil in her head like a piercing migraine. "He must have some way of seeing into my head and following when we time travel," thought Alice.

Ethan skied off to the right, following a powder trail between some trees. He waved a pole at something and disappeared into the tree line. Robert followed, steadying himself on his wolf board.

"This side, Alice! Split up!" yelled Squanto from behind.

Alice glanced over her shoulder. Squanto overtook her and veered off to the left. She followed him in and out of the trees and deeper into the forest, where a snowmobile could not follow. They were well away from the tourist ski area now. Squanto slowed down and turned his board to stop, showering Alice in fresh powder.

"Urgh! Cheers!" she said spitting snow and wiping her face.

Squanto was laughing.

"That ought to buy us a few minutes," he said.

"Where to?" panted Alice. Her heart was pounding and her legs were a bit shaky.

"You're a... how would you say it... a cool skier, Alice," said Squanto.

"Thanks. I'm not as fast as Robert. But it's a great way to get around a mountain, that's for sure. You're a good rider yourself, Squanto. The best in your century I should think! You'd be the Olympic champion!"

Squanto wiped some snow from Alice's chin.

"A Time Regent needs many skills. And many friends."

He looked at her warmly with his dark eyes.

"Alice..."

"Yes?"
"Would you..."
Before Squanto could finish, there was a loud bang.
"Explosives?" said Alice.
"Musket fire," said Squanto. "On a mountain? Idiot!"
"It might start an avalanche," said Alice.
"Exactly! This way!"
Squanto flipped his board around and they sped off again, towards a rocky outcrop further down the mountain. Alice could hear the rumble as the snow above them started to move. Squanto was making for the rocks.
"Flick, Alice!" he yelled over his shoulder.
She squeezed the totem stick, keeping her skis together. She was skiing faster than she had ever done. She tried to concentrate her thoughts on time travelling, but the thundering noise behind her and the dangerous vibrations on the mountainside were very distracting. She saw Squanto disappear. Alice was alone on a mountain in America ahead of an avalanche. For one second she felt a surge of panic. What if she time travelled to the wrong time by mistake? Out here, one girl was nothing but an insignificant speck of life in the wilderness.
She blinked the snow away. The blizzard was getting worse. She trained her thoughts on Squanto and the year 1621 and squeezed.
It worked. Alice flicked back through the years in a flash. She skidded on a mogul and bumped down the other side. She almost fell and dug the edges of her skis into the snow. She used all her might to turn them parallel and she stopped abruptly. The roar and shake of the avalanche had gone.
Squanto was standing further down the slope,

waiting for Ethan and Robert who were traversing the hillside towards him. Alice gave the mountain above her one last look and sighed deeply.

She gave a whoop of relief as she skied down to the others. They stopped by the entrance to a cave. Ethan unclipped his skis and stood them up against the rock. A low drumming sound was coming from within.

With trembling legs, Alice took off her skis.

"What happened to Captain Hunt?" she said.

Robert was grinning at her.

"He got trapped by his own stupidity," he said. "Just before Ethan and I flicked here to safety we saw him trying to outrun the avalanche."

"He's not a mountain man," said Ethan. "He's dead. Firing muskets up a mountain is a sure way of bringin' the snow down on top of you."

"Who's inside?" said Robert. He was looking at the fiery glow that danced along the walls of the narrow cave entrance. "No bears I hope!"

20

Teenage Spots

"Come on," said Squanto. "We are expected."

Massasoit, the mighty Time Regent, was sitting cross-legged by the fire, smoking a long pipe. He was dressed in white furs and leather moccasins again and his face was painted with streaks of red. The smile lines around his powerful eyes creased in laughter as he stood to greet them. Behind him stood Two Bears.

"Hello," she said.

"Hello, Two bears. Or should I say Virginia?" said Robert.

"Two Bears is my name," she said, smiling shyly. "And yours is Shadowheart."

"I don't think I want that name," said Robert.

"It is a good name for you, Robert," said Massasoit. "It is your destiny to lift the shadow from the hearts of others as a time traveller, which is a mighty quest for the powerful Regent that I think you will become."

Robert smiled slightly.

Two Bears offered him a flask.

Robert looked warily at it.

"What's in here?" he said.

"Are you afraid you may have dreams and commune with the spirits again?" said Sachem Massasoit.

"Perhaps," said Robert.

"You must trust your friends, Shadowheart," said Squanto, holding his hand out for the flask. Squanto drank greedily. He wiped his chin and passed it to Robert.

Robert looked at Squanto for a second. Then he

raised one eyebrow and his face melted into a wide grin. He lifted the flask in a toast.

"Sure. Here's to flickering . . . the coolest trick on a board I'll ever do!"

He swigged and passed the flask to Alice. The fruity drink was very refreshing.

"You have a powerful totem, Robert" said Massasoit.

Everyone looked at the sachem.

"Your totem is the great bear," said Massasoit.

Robert raised one eyebrow and grinned.

"Cool!" he said. "I'm strong, fluffy and like to sleep a lot in winter."

Everyone laughed.

"What's my totem?" said Alice.

"Epanow was right when he instinctively called you Sky Lion," said Massasoit. "Your totem is the lion. Like a lioness, you are a powerful hunter but you like to live in a friendly community."

"She certainly likes food. And that red hair, if it's not brushed, it's the image of a lion's mane," said Robert, grinning.

"It's not red. It's strawberry-blond," said Alice, scowling at him affectionately.

"Come. Sit," said Massasoit. He drew a deep breath from his pipe. "I have been busy while you were chasing around in the snow."

Squanto grinned and mimed his coolest snowboard moves at Alice. She grinned back.

"Oops. Sorry," said Squanto, bowing respectfully at his chief.

"Have you thought of a way to get the correct medicine?" said Alice.

"I have done better than that," said the sachem. He produced a pouch and opened it. It was full of tiny white pills.

"How did you do that?" said Robert. "You wouldn't steal them. Did you use magic?"

Massasoit shook his head.

"Not exactly," he said. "I read your book; your *talking tree*. I needed the help of the spirits to show me the meaning of your markings. It was very interesting. I have learned that we should mask our faces if we cough when we are ill since tiny droplets spread diseases. That is how plague is spread from man to man. The first man to begin the epidemic, like William Bradford in this case, caught the disease from infected fleas that live on the fur of rats. The rats probably came here on white men's ships, where rats would thrive in the dirty conditions. I think your ancestors will not make that simple discovery for several centuries."

"But where did you get the tetracycline?" said Robert. "That's what William needs now. It's too late too tell him about cleaning up his ship and not stepping on any rats."

"I developed spots!" said Massasoit laughing.

"Spots? Zits? Like you get on your face when you're a teenager?" said Robert, wide eyed in amazement.

"Yes! I shaved off my beard and rubbed in some roots and herbs to irritate the skin on my forehead and chin and make it seem as if I had what the medicine book calls *acne*. Then I consulted the doctor at the family practice in the twenty-first century. You see, I read in your book that, as luck would have it, tetracycline is also used to treat spots as well as plague."

"But you're an old . . . that is . . . " Robert blushed slightly. "What I mean is, you're not a teenager."

"No matter. Your book said spots could develop at any age. Besides, I am young at heart!" said

Massasoit. "The doctor was impressed with my medical knowledge. I asked for tetracycline and said I was going on holiday, so the doctor gave me a large supply. My spots soon got better when I stopped rubbing in my irritant pastes. I had to time travel back for a few months of course, to allow my beard to grow back, for I would be cold without it in the snow!"

"Brilliant!" said Alice. "You are very clever. So we can take these tablets to William Bradford?"

"Indeed. And now you must hurry," said the chief. "Ferdinando Gorges is still at large in the highways of the cosmos and could yet reach us before the treaty is signed between the pilgrims and my people. But first, you must save William."

"We need to travel to the pilgrims' encampment," said Two Bears. "Our friend Kills Eagle has scouted ahead. He has opened up the summer camp and waits for us. We must use a roving tunnel. If we journey on foot or on horseback it will take too many days to reach them."

"For the moment, my job is done," said Ethan. "I will return to my own time for a short while. There is much for me to do there to fulfill my own destiny. I will be back soon. Squanto and Massasoit can contact me in an emergency."

Massasoit nodded.

"Thank you, my friend," he said. "You have kept these travellers safe. Good luck with your own war."

Ethan saluted Massasoit and waved at Alice and Robert.

"Goodbye for now, brother," said Squanto.

In a flash Ethan was gone, as he time travelled back to his own time in a flurry of snowflakes.

"Let us go," said Massasoit. He put down his pipe and stood up. "We will travel the highways of time together. Follow my lead."

Alice held Robert's hand on one side and Squanto's on the other. Two Bears was next to Robert and Massasoit. The chief placed a small feather headdress on his head and took Squanto's hand. Alice saw that the headdress was decorated with many shells.

"This crown is a special Time Trigger. The shells have powers that enable me to see into the past and the future. They help me to concentrate my powers. We will need a large time tunnel," said Massasoit.

"We have used a shell Trigger before," said Alice. "Lady Godiva once helped us to get home with one. It was called the Shell of Destiny," said Alice.

"It may well have come into her hands from lands across the oceans at a gathering of Time Regents. Perhaps even from in this land. This America," said Massasoit.

Alice nodded. She remembered the Time Regent, Tostig, who had first shown her the Shell of Destiny. He had told her it had come into his possession on a distant shore.

"Close your eyes," said Massasoit.

He began to chant. Alice gripped Robert and Squanto's hands and began to drift. Together they travelled in a mesmerizing circle of power, floating and twisting in a tunnel of light. Alice's mind seemed to join with Massasoit's as he chanted and sang. He repeated his ancient poetry over and over. Alice could feel him pulling her along in an exotic, spiralling dance that was, in turn, happy and sad. Then he stopped his chant and Alice knew they were somewhere else. She could hear waves and smell the salty spray of the sea.

She opened her eyes.

"When and where are we?" she asked.

Squanto brushed the snow from his boots and looked around.

"The spring of 1621 in Plymouth, Massachusetts," he said. "At least that's what it will be called if we get to sign the treaty. I'll be back in a minute with horses."

He wandered off into the woods behind them.

"Is this where the first pilgrims landed?" said Robert.

"Not exactly," said Two Bears. "They first docked at Cape Cod. But that was several months ago, if I'm not mistaken. William Bradford's wife died then. Many more have since succumbed to the cold and to starvation. Nearly half of the original one hundred and two that landed here on the *Mayflower* have died in this first winter. The survivors are desperate. They may have been brave pilgrims but they were not prepared for our winters or how to grow crops on this soil."

"Is it up to us to save them all?" asked Alice.

"Yes," said Massasoit. "That is your destiny and ours. We native peoples can show them secrets to save them from starvation. You must save William, for he has a mighty part to play in the leadership of this land. It is time to take the proper medicine to William."

21

Fish Fertilizer

Squanto reappeared through the trees leading a horse. He passed the reins to Two Bears.

"I will see you at the summer camp," said Massasoit. "Squanto will show you the white man's village. Come, Two Bears."

Two Bears helped her grandfather onto his horse and led it away through the trees.

"This way," said Squanto. "Keep quiet. We will watch from a distance."

They walked up to the brow of a small hill and crawled on their hands and knees until they could just see over the top. A small village lay in the valley below. Fields had been cleared around it but nothing was growing in them. Alice could see pilgrims wandering in and out of houses. A woman in a plain dress and white cap was scrubbing at flagons and pewter plates. Two children played in a deserted courtyard. On one side was a large field filled with graves. Wooden crosses marked the mounds of cold earth. Not far away, a young man was sitting on a fallen tree. He was writing on some kind of paper. He coughed into a handkerchief.

"That's . . ." started Alice.

"Sshh!" hissed Squanto.

"Sorry," whispered Alice. "But that's William Bradford."

"I know," said Squanto.

"What's he doing?" said Robert.

"I have watched him before," said Squanto. "He writes much, like Ethan does, in a book. Perhaps

William keeps a record of these sad times for his people. He would do better to stop them wasting their time with that crop they bring from England. It will not grow if they plant it like that."

"Do you know how to help them grow food?" said Alice.

"Of course," said Squanto.

"Then you should help them," said Alice.

"If I go down there they will probably kill me with their pistols or muskets," mocked Squanto.

"I doubt it," said Alice. "Not the great and invincible Squanto!"

"O.K! O.K!" said Squanto, crossing his eyes like an idiot. "Only joking! If you keep hold of your own Triggers for now, you will stay invisible. It is better for the moment."

"Don't get too close," said Alice. "Remember what your chief told us about catching plague when people cough."

Squanto nodded. He stood up and walked towards William Bradford.

He startled the young pilgrim. William jumped up. Alice could see how thin and pale he had become.

"Oh! It's you, Squanto. It is good to see you."

"Things are bad, I think?" said Squanto.

"Very bad indeed. Our crops fail. Some of the berries have poisons in them. And this cold. This perishing cold. We are not equipped for these conditions."

"And you, my friend," said Squanto. "You do not look well."

"No. I fear for my health. Is this the beginning of the great plague?" said William. "Is this why you took me to meet those children in the church at Babworth...the ones I was warned about in my vision who would bring powerful medicine?"

Squanto looked down and touched William's journal.

"Talking trees . . ." he muttered.

"What do you mean?" said William. "I do not understand your spirits, Squanto?"

"Never mind," said Squanto. "Do you trust me?"

"Of course."

Squanto put his fingers to his mouth and gave a low wolf whistle at Robert and Alice.

"Close your eyes, William," he said. "Give me your Triggers," he added to Alice and Robert under his breath.

As soon as they released the Triggers into Squanto's hands, Alice and Robert became visible to all the people of Squanto and William's time, even those who were not time travellers.

"You can open your eyes now," said Squanto.

William blinked and stumbled.

"Where did you two come from? How did you get to this land? In another ship?"

"On a plane," said Robert.

"A what?" said William.

"Oh, never mind," said Robert. "It's a kind of ship."

"We have something that will make you well again," said Alice.

She gave him the pouch. "These are powerful medicine. Take them several times a day and you will soon be well. And don't cough on others, or you will spread the germs."

"And about these crops," said Squanto. "You'd be better with corn. And you need to catch some fish and grind it up."

"Why?" said William.

"To help the corn grow."

"Will you show us?" said William.

"Of course. When you are better."

"Come with me. I will call the elders to meet with you," said William.

"I will come," said Squanto. "But I do not think it would be wise if my two young friends were known to your people. Stay here, William, and avert your eyes. I need to talk with my friends."

He beckoned to Robert and Alice.

"Here. Take your Triggers back. You can follow when you are invisible to them," he said.

"Yes. I think it would be better," said Alice. "What will you tell William about us?"

"I'll think of something," said Squanto over his shoulder as he walked back to William.

"Have they gone?" said William, looking with unseeing eyes in the direction of Robert and Alice.

"They have other work to do," said Squanto.

"But I did not have a chance to thank them," said William. "How can I ever thank them enough anyway?"

"They don't want gold," said Squanto, giving the others a cheesy grin. "They know that you are grateful. Now. Are you going to take me to your people before I change my mind?"

William led Squanto and his two invisible followers towards the tented homes of the first pilgrims.

"Houses would last the winter if you used birch bark and bent it over to support the roof," said Squanto. "Don't worry. I will show you."

As they approached the encampment they heard shouts of alarm.

"Do not fear!" shouted William Bradford. "This man is a friend. He is one of the native peoples of this new land. He has come to help us and show us how to grow food."

William led them to a clearing with benches arranged like pews. A crowd was gathering. Squanto grinned at the pilgrim children and pulled playful faces at them.

Alice and Robert watched the proceedings from the back.

"Urgh!" said Alice. She stood on a tree stump. "Rats!"

"Nice place," said Robert.

Squanto was enjoying all the attention. Every now and again, he winked at Alice. Several of the pilgrims were introduced as they told their stories. William Brewster was there with his wife, Mary. There was a Mr Isaac Allerton with a daughter called Remember Allerton. Two children playing nearby called each other Henry and Humility. One woman carried a baby who she said she had called Oceanus because he was born during the voyage on the *Mayflower*.

"They have some weird names," whispered Alice. "And that little girl thumping her brother over there definitely shouldn't be called Humility!"

"Sshh!" said Robert. "I want to listen to what they're saying about the voyage. It sounds very exciting with storms and collapsed masts and stuff."

"Sounds grim to me," said Alice.

"...so we may see the *Mayflower's* sails any day now on the horizon," continued William Brewster. "...as she sets sail back to England."

Alice looked hopefully out to sea but the horizon was empty.

"Will none of you return on her?" said Squanto.

"No," said William Bradford. "We will succeed here, with God's grace. There is nothing for us in England. The church leaders are in the pay of the king and he wants us out because we do not bow down before him as we do before God. If you disobey the king you apparently sin against God, and if you do not worship the bishops, you commit treason. That is madness! No. Here we can be free. We come in peace. Will you help us, Squanto?"

"Indeed I will," said Squanto. "I will teach you how to dig for clams on the beaches, how to build strong houses and how to tap the maple trees for syrup. The Wampanoag people will give you corn to plant. But first we must build the earth into mounds and bury ground fish deep in each. We will plant two or three seeds in each mound. The fish will be a fertilizer and your maize will grow strong in summer."

William Bradford shook Squanto's hand.

"Now my people have hope," he said. "This is medicine indeed!"

"I must return to my chief," said Squanto, looking pleased with himself. "Take your medicine, William. And tonight your leaders may come to our village for a celebration. I will come for you."

He turned to Alice and Robert.

"Come!" he said, looking directly at them.

Robert punched Alice, who was daydreaming. She had been watching the children playing.

"Time to go," said Robert.

"At least these children won't be singing *Ring-a-ring-o-roses*," said Alice.

22

Husky

Alice ran after Robert and Squanto into the forest trail. They walked for quite a while, weaving a hidden path deep into the tall trees.

"Where are we going, Squanto?" said Robert. "This is very dark and creepy. Are there any wolves in here?"

"The Wampanoag summer camp is not far. This is a short cut," said Squanto.

They emerged into a valley. Melting snow lay in foamy pockets, dripping under the early spring sunshine. In the distance were the familiar domed houses of the Wampanoag, built in orderly rows surrounded by fields.

"Those fields will be planted when the whole tribe arrives for the summer," said Squanto.

Two Bears came out to greet them.

"It went well," said Squanto.

"Good. Massasoit was sure it would. I need to pick some herbs in the forest to accompany the meat for tonight's feast. Would you like to help me?" said Two Bears.

Robert looked interested.

"Sure. I'll come for a walk with you," he said.

"I'll come with Alice," said Squanto. He gave her a roguish smile.

"Did you see that mound of snow moving?" said Two Bears, stopping suddenly.

"Maybe there's a bear inside that's waking up," said Robert. He ran his hand up Alice's back.

"Probably just a poor racoon that saw you and

took fright," said Alice.

"That pile of snow *is* moving," said Two Bears. "The ice on the top is cracking."

"Sshh!" said Squanto.

"This really is getting a bit spooky," whispered Robert.

"Oh! You do get freaked out like normal mortals then?" said Alice sarcastically. She put her hands above her shoulders, pretending to be a ghost.

Suddenly, the snow on the top of the pile exploded. Everyone jumped. Nobody was smiling now. Alice's heart started to thump rapidly. A solitary hand pushed through the snow.

"That's not a ghost," said Squanto. "I recognise that gloved hand."

The rest of the snowy pile crumbled and Sir Ferdinando Gorges stood up. He threw off his blanket and brushed the snow from his doublet.

"That was... cool!" he sneered, fingering the Indian arrowhead Time Trigger. "Freezing in fact. But worth the wait. My blood was hot after all that time travelling to find you. I needed to cool down anyway. I could not wait around in England and die a pauper as some of your history books suggest. I almost thought I did not have the power to locate you at one point. Silly me! As if! I am the greatest Time Regent that ever lived!"

"You are certainly one of the most evil," said Two Bears. "You steal and murder in the name of your king to fuel your greed. You will never find the golden city."

"Aha! So you do know where Norumbega is," said Gorges. His eyes narrowed. "I will let you live if you lead me there."

"And you will not harm my friends either?" said Two Bears.

"Of course not. You have my word," muttered Gorges.

He took a step towards Two Bears.

Squanto spat at his feet.

"Don't be a fool, Two Bears," said Squanto.

"Yeah! Don't trust this prat," said Robert.

From the corner of her eye, Alice saw Squanto nod at Robert as his arm slid towards the knife on his belt.

Suddenly, the young men leapt towards Gorges. But it was too late. The Englishman grabbed Two Bears.

"The barn . . ." shouted Two Bears but her voice was lost as she and Gorges vanished in a silver Time Tunnel.

"Oh, great!" said Squanto, looking very annoyed. "It really is time we sorted this Gorges out once and for all! Let's go! Time Trigger please."

"Where to?" said Robert.

"Your time, I think," said Squanto. "Two Bears is cunning. She will lead Gorges into a trap. And I know where." Alice and Robert looked at him expectantly. "The barn behind the shop in Stowe. That's what she was trying to say. She'll trick him into following the trail from there. And I know why. Come on. Create a roving Time Tunnel please, Robert. You should be getting good at making these now."

Robert grinned and bent down to touch the floor with his Trigger. Alice linked arms with Squanto and reached for Robert's other hand. She closed her eyes and took breaths through alternate nostrils, calming her heartbeat and thinking of where they wanted to go. In two seconds, they were time travelling. The power of their collected thoughts pulsed through them, sending them spiralling across the ages in a racing, giant snow-twister. Alice's senses were suspended in the suction of the Time Tunnel. In her mind, she sensed the presence of other worlds across the galaxies of time.

She opened her eyes. It was snowing heavily. The street lights gave the whiteness a fiery orange glow. They were in the courtyard behind Two Bears' and Massasoit's shop. The red barn door was open. Something was whimpering inside.

To Alice's surprise, Squanto was grinning.

"She must have lost him and got the team ready," he said, walking through the barn door.

Robert shrugged at Alice. Something growled inside the barn. Then another whimper. Robert and Alice edged slowly after Squanto.

"Hello, gorgeous!" said Squanto to someone inside the barn.

Robert peered inside.

"Wolves?" he said in surprise.

"Husky dogs!" said Alice. "Six of them! They're lovely. Will they bite?"

"Only if you're mean to them," said Squanto.

He ruffled the grey fur of the lead dog. Then he whistled for Two Bears. There was no reply. The dogs barked and looked at Squanto in anticipation.

"Where is she?" said Squanto. "Where is Two Bears?"

"Not here," came a familiar voice from the doorway.

Alice turned to greet the stocky silhouette of Ethan Allen.

"I got the team ready," said Ethan. "Massasoit warned me to. He has seen Gorges and Two Bears in one of his visions. Get in. I know where they are going. Gorges still has Two Bears captive but she has got him to follow the mountain trail in this century. He thinks that Norumbega is across the shores of Lake Champlain. Two Bears has tricked him that there is a golden city there. In a way, she is right. New York State is on the other side. What greater claim can any earthly place have than New York for the title of golden city?"

"Ha! I see your point," said Robert. "A city like London. Dick Whittington, in one of our English stories, thought the streets of London would be paved with gold."

"Precisely," said Squanto. "Massasoit says the real golden city lies within us."

"The new Jerusalem," muttered Ethan with a distant look in his eyes. He tutted and shrugged. "William Bradford would understand. I think I shall write a philosophy book for the Americans of my time when this is over. Come on. Let's go. I know the route Two Bears will take across the foothills. She knows we can overtake them in the sledge."

Alice climbed into the fur-lined sledge and sat down behind Robert, stretching her legs on either side of him. Squanto sat behind her. Ethan stood on the back and took the reins.

The dogs barked in a frenzy, sensing their imminent departure. With a jolt, the sledge was moving, gliding on the ice in the courtyard and out into the falling snow.

"Wicked!" shouted Robert.

Alice had to agree. It was breathtaking. The smooth runners slid over the snow and tilted as the dogs raced around bends. Sometimes Alice thought the sledge might tip over and they would be thrown out. But Ethan was an expert driver. The dogs yelped in delight, their strong bodies pulling as one.

Alice looked over the sides of the sledge when the driving snow was less stinging on her face. They sped past a frozen swimming pool. Like the great frozen lakes, the heavy snowfall lay thick on the ice, camouflaging the pit below in a deceptive white blanket. Alice could only recognise the swimming pool by the silver handrails of the pool steps that arched from the smooth white icing. The dogs pulled harder as they began to climb parallel to the road, leaving the town behind them. Alice could just make out the silhouette of the wooden rafters of the covered bridge where, according to the notes she had read in the hotel reception, a jilted bride had once thrown herself to her doom in the icy currents below.

Alice couldn't help thinking they were like the brave puritans and first white trappers. They were penetrating a vast wilderness now. This was frontier country. Two Bears' homeland was the reluctant witness to many massacres and bloody struggles. She knew that the daily fight for survival of the animals and plants was mirrored in the human violence carried out on its soil in the name of freedom. She suspected that even those that came in peace might one day turn on allies in a human quest to own and rule.

Alice shuddered and pulled the fur blanket closer. The icy wind was burning any exposed skin and she buried her face in Robert's back.

The sledge slowed and stopped. The canopy of trees above them afforded an umbrella against the blizzard.

"Where are we?" said Robert.

"Sshh!" whispered Squanto.

Alice could see that Ethan was keeping the dogs as quiet and still as possible. Squanto edged himself out of the back of the sledge and examined the ground and undergrowth around them with Ethan.

"This should do it," whispered Squanto as he got

back in behind Alice. "He's trapped."
"Where?" said Robert.
"Between us and the lake," said Squanto. "You'll see."

23

Thanksgiving

Ethan Allen whispered something to the dogs. They were surprisingly quiet now. Slowly, Ethan guided the sledge in a semi-circle to the edge of the clump of trees. Alice blinked through the snow and thought she could see a shape moving in the darkness on the slope ahead.

Suddenly, Squanto whooped and shouted. Ethan jerked at the reins and the sledge shot forwards, advancing on the shapes ahead. The blizzard was thinning now and the violet sky sparkled with stars.

"It's Gorges and Two Bears!" shouted Robert. "They're on snowshoes."

Sir Ferdinando Gorges turned, startled by the sudden noise.

"Look out for his fire stick!" yelled Squanto.

Gorges grabbed Two Bears in an arm lock. He pushed her in front of him as a human shield and aimed his musket.

Squanto whooped and the dogs howled. It was a terrible, blood-curling sound and Gorges took a step back. The sledge hurtled towards him.

At that moment, Two Bears vanished in a time travelling flash. Alice saw the flash of anger on Gorges' face. He stepped back again.

"That's it," murmured Ethan. "Just a few more steps . . ."

It was then that Alice saw it. Like the swimming pool in Stowe, she recognised the soft contours around Sir Gorges. He was standing on the frozen lake. Just behind him, the contour of the snow changed from the smoothness of regal icing to the texture of a sugar-frosted doughnut. The thinner ice was melting there and Sir Ferdinando Gorges was only two steps away.

Ethan, Squanto and Robert yelled a war cry all together. It was enough. Gorges saw the danger but it was too late. As he took his final step, the ice cracked loudly. Terror flashed across his face as he disappeared into the yawning depths below. The ice moved again, closing above him.

Alice closed her eyes and held her breath as the sledge, too, hurtled forwards towards the thinner ice. She felt Squanto's arms tighten around her as he braced his body in anticipation.

The ice cracked further but the dogs responded to Ethan's driving and their own instincts. The sledge tilted dangerously, sparking when the sides touched the frozen ground as it turned away and shot towards the mountainside.

Alice did not look back. She knew Sir Ferdinando Gorges was dead. No-one could survive in the freezing winter waters of Lake Champlain. All the way back, she clung to Robert in silence. No one spoke.

Alice was relieved to see the twinkling lights of Stowe. Two Bears was waiting in the courtyard in the doorway of the red barn. She steadied the huskies.

"Thank God you're safe," said Robert. "Did you have a secret Time Trigger?"

"Picking Gorges' pocket was easy," said Two Bears, smiling. She held out her hand. The Indian arrowhead nestled in her palm. "The token of my ancestors can rest now," she said.

"I feel suddenly peaceful," said Alice.

"The quest is done," said Ethan, returning from

settling the husky dogs in the barn. "Our enemies are vanquished and the future of the pilgrims is secure, now that William Bradford is well and the Wampanoag are teaching them how to survive. America's history is protected for now. Until the next quest and another threat."

"Yes. In that case, my friends, I think it is time to go to a party," said Squanto. He grinned mischievously. "Massasoit will be waiting."

"Are we invited?" said Robert.

"Of course!" said Squanto. "Let's go! Two Bears, a roving Time Tunnel to the autumn of 1621, if you please."

They all held hands. In a flash of white that sent the snow into a flume of powder, they were time travelling again. This time, Alice relaxed and enjoyed the ride. She let her mind snuggle with the others as they used their powers to take them exactly where they wanted to go. Too soon, it was over and Alice opened her eyes.

It was night. Native people stood with pilgrims around a massive fire. Some were singing chants of ancient beauty to the rhythm of the drums. Children played and women of both peoples joined together, putting the finishing touches to the great feast. The tantalizing smell of roast venison and wild turkey mingled with the scent of berries.

"Try this," said Two Bears. She had scooped something sweet smelling from a jar on a stick and rolled it in the snow. "It's fresh maple syrup, a modern Vermont delicacy after a sleigh ride. It is a custom from the future that I shall teach to my people of this time. I believe it is called *sugar on snow.*"

"It's fantastic," said Alice. "The best iced lolly ever!"

Massasoit walked over to greet them.

"Well done!" he said. "There were moments when I felt your peril. You were very brave."

"This is some party," said Robert. His dirty features shone red and purple in the flickering firelight.

"We have signed the treaty," said Massasoit. "This is the celebration of the first great harvest. It is a giving of great thanks. Our two peoples will be at peace for fifty years in this region, if all goes well. That is a very strong treaty."

"I'm starving. When do we eat?" said Robert.

"Now," said Massasoit. "You must first return the Time Triggers. The totem stick and the Spirit Pond rune stone will remain with the treasures of our tribe. Their job is done and the people of this time will not be able to see you while you hold them, anyway."

"How will we get back to our own time?" said Alice, passing her Trigger to the great chief.

"With this," said Squanto. His smiling eyes betrayed his fondness for her. He stepped forwards and passed Alice the dream catcher he had made for her. "You forgot it earlier."

"Oh, yes! I'm so sorry. Thank you," said Alice. She hugged Squanto and he held her close for several moments.

"Right. Party time!" said Robert. Alice grinned at him and he winked back at her.

William Bradford walked across to greet them. Alice recognised Epanow and Kills Eagle too, embracing Squanto and Ethan. Everyone walked across to enjoy the festival.

"Thank you," said William Bradford.

He shook Robert and Alice's hands.

"No sweat. It was cool," said Robert, shrugging.

"Perhaps you will return to the church at Babworth and say a prayer for us there," said William. "Go in spring when the bluebells are out. It is a sanctuary of great beauty then."

"I think we will," said Alice.

"You *can* change destiny," said Massasoit, seating himself cross-legged on his favourite rug and puffing on his pipe. "But it will never be easy."

"Have you seen our futures too?" said Alice.

The great chief smiled.

"You will face great dangers, Alice and Robert," said Massasoit. "The future is never certain. Time travellers cannot ever totally relax. But for now, it is time to rest a while."

"Come on," said Robert. "This is the very first Thanksgiving party!" He passed Alice a flagon and a pewter plate.

Alice nodded. She walked towards the warmth of the fire and the rhythm of the music.

That night, as she lay awake in the comfort of her hotel bed, Alice Hemstock, novice Time Regent, smiled to herself. This was the best holiday she could remember and if Massasoit was right, there were plenty of adventures still to come.